P9-CEM-097

Stir It Up!

Stir It Up!

A Novel

RAMIN GANESHRAM

SCHOLASTIC PRESS

NEW YORK

Copyright © 2011 by Ramin Ganeshram

All rights reserved. Published by Scholastic Press, an imprint of Scholastic Inc., *Publishers since 1920*. SCHOLASTIC, SCHOLASTIC PRESS, and associated logos are trademarks and/or registered trademarks of Scholastic Inc.

No part of this publication may be reproduced, stored in a retrieval system, or transmitted in any form or by any means, electronic, mechanical, photocopying, recording, or otherwise, without written permission of the publisher. For information regarding permission, write to Scholastic Inc., Attention: Permissions Department, 557 Broadway, New York, NY 10012.

CIP information available

Recipes on pages 79, 102, 139, 148, 161, and 163 are reproduced from *Sweet Hands: Island Cooking from Trinidad & Tobago*, second edition, by Ramin Ganeshram. Copyright © 2006, 2010 by Ramin Ganeshram. Reprinted by permission from Hippocrene Books, Inc.

ISBN: 978-0-545-16582-2

10 9 8 7 6 5 4 3 2 1   11 12 13 14 15
Printed in the United States of America 23
First edition, August 2011

The text type was set in 13-pt. Cochin Medium.
The display type was set in Dalliance Roman,
and Cooperplate Gothic BT Bold.
Book design by Marijka Kostiw

For Sophie Lollie,

my best sous chef

and my shining beacon:

May you realize your dreams

in magnificent ways.

A Note to Readers

When preparing any kind of recipe, make sure to thoroughly wash your hands before and after handling food. Clean all surfaces and utensils that have come into contact with uncooked poultry, fish, or meats. Consumption of undercooked poultry, fish, or meats can result in serious illness requiring medical attention. When defrosting poultry, fish, or meats, place in a refrigerator overnight rather than leaving out at room temperature. Only prepare recipes with the help and supervision of an adult. Never handle knives or other sharp utensils without adult supervision.

PART

ONE

BE WHO YOU ARE

Be Who You Are Bread

2 cups sharing

1 cup love

1 tablespoon essence of warmth, divided

3/4 cup comfort, for seasoning

1 cup confidence, plus extra for kneading

1. In a large bowl, sift together sharing and love.

2. Add 1 tablespoon of the essence of warmth and mix well. Stir in the comfort until combined.

3. Stir in the confidence slowly, mixing well until the mixture forms a stiff dough.

4. Turn the dough onto a clean work surface, dusted with a little extra confidence, and knead until the dough is smooth and elastic, without any holes. The dough should be firm and unbreakable.

5. Put the dough back in the bowl and place in a warm, dry location to rise until double its size.

6. Remove from the bowl, knead again gently, and bake until golden brown, firm, and delicious. Be Who You Are Bread can last indefinitely in the right environment.

CHAPTER ONE

Hustle

My heart pounds as I race around the kitchen with Deema, filling orders, trying not to get behind. It's a race that only we can win.

"Start the *pholouries*!" my father yells.

We are a jumble of bees — buzzing, bumping into each other, building something sweet and solid. Our tiny kitchen is our hive, and I feel like the busiest bee of all, working every bit of my wings to stay with the other workers — Deema and my dad. The air is thick with the smell of the different curries simmering on the stove. These spices are Deema's perfume. Her clothing and hair and even her skin are always rich with the sweet aroma. On me, the curries take on a thick mix of sweat and baby lotion and my favorite mango shampoo. It doesn't matter that Deema bleaches our aprons and my T-shirts in the laundry. I give my collar a sniff. Sure enough, I'm a walking curry cabinet.

The steam in our kitchen brings heat and wet to my face. There's a sheen on my forehead and cheeks and arms. My throat is like sandpaper, but who has time for even a gulp of water with my dad at the cash register, yelling back, "Hurry, Anjali! Customers not wanting to wait!"

Deema's hot, too, but she keeps moving. With the tail of her apron she pats the moisture from her neck each time she approaches the stove. I run my knuckles over my forehead.

I drop the *pholouries* into the fryer basket, jumping back when oil splashes and burns me with its hot droplets. The balls of dough bubble in the oil, and I pull them out as they turn light golden brown.

"*Pholouries* ready!" I yell.

I manage to gulp a sip of water. Even though it's tepid, the wet meets my throat and brings the promise of relief to my insides. My stomach is grateful for the water, but it calls to me with a sharp *grrruuurrrahhhh*. I'm reminded that cooks don't stop to eat while preparing, even though I'm hungry enough to down every bit of dough in the middle of this busy hive. But if I stop, even for a moment, I won't be able to keep up.

"Quick, Anjali!" calls Deema. "Get more *pholourie* dough from the refrigerator."

The water in my belly sloshes and mixes with the *grrruuurrrahhh* as I reach into the fridge to pull out a tray of ground lentils and spices with both my arms. The push of cold coming from the fridge is a relief as it quick-dries my sweaty face.

Deema is holding a knife, thumb securely on its handle — chop-chopping so fast, in a blur. She considers me for a moment. "Don't just stand there — get those *pholouries* in the oil, girl, and while they are frying get another knife."

I follow and start in on an onion, slow at first. It doesn't take long for the onion sting to meet my eyes and force tears. I wipe my eyes with the bottom of the apron and focus. I chop steadily until I am moving almost as fast as Deema, who taught me how to use a knife back when I was eight by embracing me from the back to help me chop-chop. I smile as I remember being enfolded in her arms, hard muscle from years of work within soft skin, hugging me, taming back the onion sting. Together, we chop, and the smell of her curry perfume mixes with my own curry and shampoo. The knives and our hands move like twins, working fast to turn the onion into a mound of tiny white spicy pieces. "Good work," Deema encourages.

I take up a new knife, a smaller one. "I have an idea," I tell Deema. "One that doesn't involve onions."

Deema nods. "Okay, but easy does it."

I dash over to a tray of freshly fried bakes sitting by the stove, waiting to be wrapped up with an order of salted spiced codfish or mashed pumpkin. I slit the side of each small savory bread open, working as fast as I can so the steam that puffs out of them doesn't burn my fingers. I smooth pink guava jam over the bottom of each one, then close up the sandwich. To finish, I sprinkle superfine sugar and cinnamon on top of each. The bakes are still hot as I work. I lick my fingers to coax back the steam burns. The sugar and cinnamon melt nicely when they hit each fritter's surface. I smile at the warm smell of the cinnamon, though my stomach is still making its noise.

I put one of my creations on a small plate and bring it over to Deema, who looks at it, then at me, and smiles. She holds a metal bowl under the table and uses her hand to scoop the chopped onions inside. She sets aside the bowl and wipes her hand, picking up my creation with two fingers so it doesn't get oniony. Finally, Deema takes a bite of my invention. She closes her eyes as she chews and considers the flavors.

"Anjali, this is lovely!"

Deema knows good cooking when she tastes it. But we have little time to enjoy my creativity.

Up front in the restaurant, my father is taking more orders. The place is getting packed. "Anjali, come!" he calls. "I need help wrapping the rotis."

I untie my oil-splattered apron, grab a new one from the cubby near the register, and put it on. Customers don't want to see me dirty while I wrap up their food.

This is a typical sort of evening for my family. Me, Dad, Deema, sometimes my mom, and usually never my brother, Anand, take turns working in our roti shop, Island Spice, in Richmond Hill, Queens, where we live along with a million other Trinidadians and Guyanese families. On a busy night like this, it feels like every one of them comes through our shop.

It's hard work, but I love it better than anything because I get to try out my own culinary experiments whenever I want. I guess you could say that cooking is my hobby. Well, at least that's what my parents and teachers call it. But *hobby* is a lame word. For me, food is my soul's work. My dream is to be the youngest Food Network chef by the time I'm fifteen. That means I have two years to make it happen. I want to have my own show about Caribbean food. No one has done that yet. I'll be the first. There's a lot more to Caribbean cooking than jerk chicken. In Trinidad, we've got more kinds of food than anyone could imagine. Our main specialty is curry, and I'm ready to show that to all my viewers once I get the TV spotlight.

I've even got the name of my show all worked out: *Cooking with Anjali Krishnan*, or *The Curry Kitchen with Anjali Krishnan*.

But for now my only show is *showing up* for my family in this beehive of a shop.

I'm deep in the dream of my own TV show when someone calls, "Hey, Anjali, darlin', how you goin'?"

I look up and smile at Mr. Farrell, an old Trinidadian man who has come to the restaurant

8

nearly every night for his supper since his wife died a few years back.

"Hello, Mr. Farrell," I say, smiling. "What can I get you tonight?"

"Ah . . . let me see." He glances around at the trays behind the counter. "What's good?"

"The dumplings and cassava are real nice tonight, and there's some stew chicken," I answer.

"Yes, that will be fine. Plenty pepper, okay?"

"Yes, sir," I reply. "Staying with us this evening?" I really don't have to ask. Mr. Farrell almost never does takeout. Mr. Farrell eats at one of the tables and watches people come and go, sometimes staying for a long time after he's finished eating. Mr. Farrell likes our shop because we don't play our music too loud and, instead of all the usual *soca* concert posters, our walls are covered with photos of Trinidad that my dad took himself. Our customers look at the pictures for a long time while they wait for their orders. Dad's pictures remind them of home.

Outside, my father has the red, black, and white flag of Trinidad on one side of the door, the American flag on the other. Dad has hung the American flag just slightly higher up — about two inches. This is part of what he calls, "Doin' right, walkin' good, speakin' true," which means doing the right thing. As far as flags go, a country's flag is always highest in its own land. My father is very particular about things like that.

I grab a plate for Mr. Farrell and pile it high with chicken, dumplings, and cassava cooked in a light curry. I spoon some of Deema's special homemade pepper sauce — reserved for the best customers, everyone else gets bottled — and sprinkle it over the food. It's yellow and thick, and the sharp bite of the Scotch bonnet peppers is so strong I feel a catch and tickle in my throat just from the vapors alone.

I reach into one of the foil-covered trays that holds another one of my creations — a salad I've made from shredded jicama, arugula, sliced avocado, and mango that I've dressed with seasoned rice vinegar, toasted sesame oil, and sesame seeds. The salad isn't truly Trinidadian, but Dad lets me give out my "specials" to our best customers, or those who know us well and are willing to be tasters. Mr. Farrell definitely qualifies as a taster. Besides, I feel sorry for

Mr. Farrell. He seems so lonely. When I make up his plate, I add something extra — usually one of my experiments. I put together a small plate of the salad for Mr. Farrell. The toasted sesame is savory and smoky, and makes the mango taste brighter and sweeter.

I bring out the tray to Mr. Farrell, who is already sitting. He smiles.

"Thank you, darlin'," he says, squinting at the salad. "What's this?"

"A salad I'm experimenting with. I thought you might give me your opinion."

"Happy to!" Mr. Farrell says, scooting his chair close to his plate. "Anjali, child, those stuffed callaloo leaves you gave me the other day were just delicious!"

I smile. "Thanks," I say, knowing he's telling the truth. Most of my experiments are delicious. I quickly return to the back of the counter, to help Dad steadily fill orders. Our place is still packed with hungry people.

An hour passes with customers coming in nonstop. When it finally quiets down, Dad tells me,

"Anjie, I goin' fuh me supper." In the back, Deema has our own dinner already set up. She's been waiting for my father to join her.

Mr. Farrell's plate is empty. He's eaten every morsel. I go over to clear his table.

"Enjoy your meal?" I ask politely.

"As always," Mr. Farrell says happily. "Delicious salad, Anjali. I must steal your recipe." He chuckles, then he leans over and points his finger at me. "You, my girl, is a born cook!"

CHAPTER TWO

Pow

The next day I stare into the case at Fat Moon, the Chinese bakery down the street from my school. I've been meaning to check out this place since school started last month. I figure I deserve a little treat after all the activity last night at our roti shop.

"What's in those?" I ask the lady behind the counter.

"They're bean cakes filled with a paste made of beans," she answers in a heavy New York accent.

"Hmmm." I walk the length of the counter, staring at these cakes, each about the size of a hockey puck. There are also little tarts filled with what looks like vanilla pudding, and round buns, golden brown, about the size of a softball.

"What about these?" I say, pointing at the buns.

"They got roast pork in them," she answers.

Over by the door my best friend, Lincoln Courtnay, sighs. "Come *on*, Anjali," he calls impatiently. "We're going to be late." He hikes his knapsack farther up his shoulder, rumpling his school blazer.

"Okay, okay," I say, and quickly give my order. "I'll take one of the pork buns and one of those bean cakes."

The woman behind the counter puts them in a brown paper bag and rings me up.

"Three dollars," she says, holding her hand out while I dig into the front pocket of my knapsack to find a five-dollar bill. I grab my change and run out to the sidewalk where Lincoln is waiting.

"Check these out, Linc!" I say, reaching into the bag. "It's *pow* and Chinese cake!" That's what we call cakes like this in Richmond Hill.

"Yeah, so?" he says, walking quickly down Queens Boulevard, away from Fat Moon Bakery and toward Forest Hills School on Union Turnpike, three blocks away.

I run next to Linc, trying to match his stride. He can't seem to remember that we aren't the same size anymore, and it's hard for me to keep up. Linc is already nearly five feet nine, when just last year, in seventh grade, we were still close to the same height.

I'm only five feet tall, and now I feel like a little kid when I stand next to Linc.

I pull the pork bun out of the bag. "Don't you think it's funny that China is on the other side of the world from Trinidad and they have the same kinds of food we do?" I shove the pork bun at him. "Here, eat this one."

Linc says, "I'm not hungry now. I just ate lunch."

"I know, but I need to know what a pork roll tastes like, and you know I can't eat pork," I say. "They didn't have the chicken or vegetable ones like we do."

Linc sighs and stops walking. He's used to being my personal taster, but just to bug me he likes to pretend tasting bothers him. Deep down, Linc likes to try out new foods.

Linc's my taster a lot, especially when I want to find out about some new food that I'm not allowed to eat. My family is Hindu, so stuff with beef and pork is totally off-limits for me. When I'm a famous TV chef I'll have a staff of tasters, but for now Linc's the one with the taste buds.

He takes the bun from me and carefully peels back the square of white parchment paper at its bottom. He gently breaks the bun in half. Slices of roasted pork covered in dark red sauce drip out. Linc quickly nibbles a piece.

"Yeah, it's *pow*," he says.

I slap him a high five. "Cool! Let me try this bean cake — you want some?" Linc shakes his head. He looks annoyed, like he's eager to get going already. But I'm all about the cakes right now.

When I bite into the bean cake, it tastes just the same as the Chinese bean cakes we have in the bakeries in my neighborhood. "I have to ask my grandmother about this when I get home," I say.

Linc's only half listening.

"We better get going," he says. When we hear the buzzer sound in the yard of our school, Linc stuffs the rest of the pork bun into his mouth as we run to our school's front door.

"Hey, I thought you weren't hungry," I say, laughing.

"Well, yuh can't let good food, especially a pork bun, go tuh waste!" he says, imitating our parents' West Indian accent. Linc's father is one of the most prominent physicians in the city, and even he sometimes speaks in the Trini patois that is just regular speech for my parents and grandmother.

"Meet on the steps after school!" Linc calls out, heading toward his music class.

"Yep!" I race to Social Studies at the opposite end of the building.

By the time I get to class, Mr. Yan has already started his lesson on the California gold rush. He pauses when I come in. I mouth, "I'm sorry" and head to my desk. To get to my seat I have to walk by Nirmala Singh and Sunita Kumar, who roll their eyes at each other and giggle as I ease into my seat. Nirmala and Sunita are the leaders of a pack of "cool" kids, mostly Indian, some Chinese and Korean. Nirmala, who is small, dark, and not so pretty, is in charge. Sunita, who is tall and slender with light skin and big eyes, is always trailing behind Nirmala like a lapdog. When Nirmala isn't around, Sunita can be nice, but that doesn't happen often. Usually, they're together and always have something nasty to say to me about not being "real Indian," or they like to rag on me because I'm a partial-scholarship student since my parents don't have a lot of money.

When I finally reach my desk I sit down, slip my notebook and pen out of my bag as quickly as possible, and scribble down the notes Mr. Yan has written on the board. Ahead of me, down the row, I see Nirmala pushing her notebook to the edge of her desk so Sunita can read a note written in the bottom corner of the right-hand page. I shake my head. *How can Mr. Yan not see that?* Nirmala and Sunita sit right in front of him.

"Do you disagree with my assessment, Ms. Krishnan?" Mr. Yan says, looking at me.

"Uh . . . no, no, sir." My face goes hot. "I was just shaking my head at something I was thinking."

"Okay, Anjali, but try to *think* about the lesson at hand."

I nod miserably. I feel bad about not listening because Mr. Yan is one of my nicest teachers. But I am also angry at myself for giving Nirmala and Sunita something more to laugh at. Nirmala and Sunita giggle, looking over their shoulders at me.

I quickly look down. I pretend to be absorbed in writing notes, but I'm really writing *I hate N&S* over and over.

It's hard to understand why they're so mean. What

do they care where my parents were born? Nirmala and Sunita were born right here in Queens, just like I was. Doesn't that make us all the same? The African American students and even the few kids actually *from* Africa never seem to give Linc a hard time, or tell him he isn't "really" black, even though he's lighter skinned than they are, and also West Indian.

Whenever Nirmala and Sunita start up, I think about my mom, who is mixed African and Indian. She doesn't feel like she doesn't belong. She was raised in Trinidad, where Deema says "everybody mix up." So it's different for Mom. She accepts who she is.

The bell signaling the end of class can't come soon enough. This is my last period today with Nirmala and Sunita, and that's something to look forward to.

Linc and I walk across the playground before heading home. He listens patiently like he always does while I complain about Nirmala and Sunita.

"Why don't you just ignore them?" He slows his pace to match mine.

"I try, Linc, but they are just so vicious."

"They've got nothing on you, Anj. No *pow* in those two." Linc always knows how to make me smile. "*Pow*-less."

I giggle. "Later, Linc."

I cut across the playground to Austin Street behind the school to get the Q10 bus down to Liberty Avenue.

I walk through the fading sunlight, crunching the piles of fallen leaves on the sidewalk. The air is thick, sweet. Afternoon has turned the redbrick apartment buildings to glowing orange. The changing leaves make even my street, which runs right next to the Van Wyck Expressway, look pretty. Here in Forest Hills the smell of fireplace smoke from the small Tudor-style houses rises up Austin Street. At this time of year people have pumpkins and chrysanthemums on their small porches.

Whenever I walk down this street I wonder what it would be like to live in this neighborhood. It's so peaceful here. At my house the only quiet I get is late at night, when there are fewer cars on the expressway. That's when we can open our windows without hearing the constant sound of traffic.

The bus comes quickly. I squeeze on with the commuters from Manhattan. In a few stops I'm able to get a seat, so I pull out a small notebook from the front pocket of my knapsack and begin to write.

I'm still thinking about that bean cake. *It might be fun to make a pudding from the filling, but how?* I stare out the window at the traffic. It's already starting to get dark. I go back to my recipe and think some more about how I can make my own special pudding.

When I get home, I'll go to Sybil's Bakery in my neighborhood and get some more bean cakes to taste the filling again, and to really look at it, too. And I'll ask Deema — she'll definitely have some ideas.

I am so caught up in vanilla, coconut milk, and cassava beans that I almost miss my stop. I shove my way through the standing passengers before hurtling through the door and onto the sidewalk at the base of the elevated A train platform at Liberty Avenue. I stop a minute to catch my breath before walking down Liberty to my family's roti shop. The train clatters overhead, adding to the sweet mix that has now taken me over. *Vanilla. Coconut milk. Beans.* As soon as I get home, I'm in the kitchen, looking for ways to bring my pudding alive.

"What yuh doin', child?" Deema comes up from behind. I've pulled ingredients from our fridge and cupboards.

I tell her about the *pow* and the Chinese cakes.

"Ah," she says. "Sweet goodness from bitter times." Deema explains that the Chinese indentured laborers in Trinidad and Guyana brought those cakes over with them from China.

"They came even before our people did," Deema says. She goes to the bookcase in her room and returns with a book about the history of Trinidad. "Those original recipes didn't change much, even though ours did."

I look over Deema's shoulder at a picture of Chinese men cutting stalks of sugarcane.

Deema is tall, slender, and stylish. She doesn't look like the other Trinidadian grandmas I know. Her skin is the color of coffee with milk. Her eyes are green. Everyone else in the family calls her Rosie, a nickname her uncle gave her back home in Trinidad when she was a baby on account of her light complexion and pink cheeks. I call her Deema, which is short for *dadeema*, the Hindu word for grandma.

"I was thinking, Deema, of trying to make a pudding that is sort of like the bean filling in those cakes, but that you could eat with a spoon."

Deema smiles widely. "Anjali, you know what's good, girl." I feel a tingle in my stomach. Deema hunts down a bag of kidney beans from the freezer, where she keeps the beans after she soaks them in water to make them soft. "I've never liked those canned beans," she says. She hands me the bag.

"Anjali, defrost these in some boiling water, then grind them up."

I boil a pot of water. Steam starts rising off of it, clouding the kitchen windows. I'm like that steam, rising with the joy that comes from cooking.

"Let's put a little piece of cassava in to make it more puddingy," says Deema.

"Cassava?" I say doubtfully, looking at the long brown root sitting in a basket on the counter.

"Yes, child," says Deema, smiling. "What you think they make tapioca from — cassava. And tapioca not only a pudding but a thickener for pies and such."

"Deema, no one knows more about cooking than you."

"Well, me ain' know 'bout *that*," Deema says, laughing. Whenever my grandmother gets excited she slips into a deeper Trinidadian accent, as sweet and as thick as the bean steam that's filled our kitchen.

I peel half a cassava and cut it into chunks, then rinse it in cold water before dumping it with the beans into the boiling pot. The beans do somersaults in the simmering water, bumping lightly against the cassava pieces. Once they're soft, I drain them in a colander and put them in the food processor.

Deema sets out some light brown sugar, which I add along with mixed essence, a flavoring that goes into most Caribbean baked things. I uncap the mixed essence and take a deep whiff before adding it in. Mixed essence smells like a mix of pears, almonds, and vanilla. It's one of my favorite smells in the world.

I cover the food processor, pulsing the beans until they start to get mashed under the blades.

"Add a little of the cooking water if you have to," Deema says to me, and hands over a small measuring cup with water she kept aside from the beans. I add it, bit by bit, through the funnel of the processor until, finally, the beans whir into a smooth pink paste.

Deema's hand is on her hip as she stares at the cupboard. "Now, let's see what else . . ."

"I was thinking coconut milk, maybe, to make it light and creamy," I say.

"You thinkin' right, Anjali," Deema says, smiling at me.

We spend the next hour making the pudding. When it's done I arrange some in a white bowl and garnish it with cinnamon. I put the bowl on a colorful place mat, then I run back to my room to get my camera to take a photo for my portfolio. Afterward, Deema and I bring some in to my mom, who is sitting at the dining room table just outside the kitchen, studying for her nursing exam.

Mom was a nurse back in Trinidad. When she came here, she had to take a bunch of new classes and retake all the tests. When she had me and Anand, she stopped studying for a while, then when we got big enough, she had to work to help my dad get the roti shop started. Now she goes to school at night, and she'll probably graduate next year.

On the other side of our L-shaped living room, my brother is doing his homework. I put some of the pudding on the coffee table in front of him and set some down for Mom, too. Back in the kitchen, I put more pudding in a bowl covered in plastic for my dad to eat when he comes in from the restaurant.

"Delicious!" Mom murmurs without looking up. "You are a culinary genius, Rosie," she says to Deema.

"Actually, Lottie, this delicious pudding was Anjali's idea," Deema says, putting her arm around my shoulders.

Mom doesn't answer. She's deep in her nursing books. Deema hugs me. She must have felt something tighten. I'm often invisible to Mom. Even my pudding can't soften her when she's studying.

Mom almost never has time to pay attention to me or Anand. She's always tired when she gets home from her nanny job taking care of the Sovald kids in Manhattan. At night she has to study. When I was a little kid, I used to think she liked those little white Sovald kids better than me and Anand, and that by the end of the day she had used up all the affection she had on them.

"Mommy don't mean nothin' by it, child," Deema starts to say as I begin pouring the rest of the pudding into a Tupperware container to take to school, where I'll share some with Linc.

"It's okay, Deema, I know," I say quickly, and put the container in the fridge before cleaning up.

Anjali's Red Bean Pudding

1 three-inch piece of cassava (yucca), peeled
1 fifteen-ounce can dark red kidney beans
1 cup water
1 cup light brown sugar
1 cup coconut milk
1 teaspoon mixed essence or vanilla extract
1/8 teaspoon nutmeg
whipped cream for garnish (optional)

1. Place the cassava in a saucepan, cover with water, and bring to a boil. Cook until fork tender, about 20 minutes.
2. When the cassava is fork tender, drain it and set aside to cool. Rinse the kidney beans in a colander and place in a large saucepan with 1 cup water and the sugar and bring to a simmer.
3. Once the cassava is cool, cut it in half

and remove the woody center. Chop into small pieces and add to the bean mixture.

4. Allow the beans to simmer until the liquid is reduced by three-quarters. Pour the mixture into a food processor and puree until smooth.

5. Return the bean mixture to the pan and add the coconut milk, mixed essence or vanilla, and nutmeg. Stir well and continue to cook over low heat until thickened further, about 5 to 10 minutes.

6. Remove and place in a heatproof bowl to cool. Chill in the refrigerator. Serve in pudding bowls or champagne flutes with whipped cream for garnish.

Makes 6 servings

CHAPTER THREE

Bustle

Island Spice is already hopping when I come in the front door. The place is always frantic on Friday nights. To get to the kitchen, I have to squeeze by customers filling up the tables in the front of the shop. In addition to the usual strong smell of curry, I can make out the smoky smell of boiling banana leaves. That means Deema is making either *pastelles* or *paymee*, a cake made out of grated cassava, coconut, and sugar, wrapped in a banana leaf.

"Dad!" I call out to my father, who is working the register. I head toward the kitchen in the back, where Deema is frying up *aloo* pies, hot potato turnovers, a favorite weekend snack around here.

I grab one of the pies, quickly moving it from hand to hand so I won't get burned, then lean over and peck Deema on the cheek.

"God bless you, *bayti*," Deema says, calling me the Hindi word for daughter. "How school was today?"

"Linc loved the red bean pudding," I say, reaching into my bag and taking out the empty Tupperware container.

Deema continues to steadily drop the prepared *aloo* pies in the deep fryer. I quickly finish my own *aloo* pie, which is spicy with hot pepper and sweet with fried onions, wipe my hands on a paper towel, tie on an apron, and head over to the sink to wash the utensils there. I'm back in the beehive. Busy. Buzzing. Cooking. Rushing. "Move it!" Dad calls.

My insides churn as I wash the various pots and pans and large spoons that Deema uses to mix the curry. Dad's voice is a drill. "Come, make it happen!" Deema steps away from the fryer to put the meals together for the waiting customers.

"One curry chicken!" Dad shouts the order. "And one *dalpuri* and curry shrimp," he calls out. Deema fills a foil takeaway container with the chicken on one side and a pile of the softly shredded rotis on the other. She covers it and puts it on the table behind her for Dad to pick up. Next she places the *dalpuri*, a roti stuffed with powdery ground yellow split peas in its folds, on a large square of parchment paper, then spoons the curry shrimp inside. She folds the whole thing into a fat square, twisting the ends of the parchment tightly so it can be eaten like a burrito.

I wash dishes faster so I can hurry to help Deema. My grandmother is fast and looks much younger than her age, but she's still an old lady and it isn't really right for her to have to run around so much, especially when Anand can help. Part of the problem is that my parents won't make Anand work in the restaurant. "He a young boy," my dad likes to say. "He need to run around and have some fun."

Whenever I bring up the subject with Mom, she sighs and says she can't think about it now or that she has to study.

Doesn't it matter that *I* don't have any fun? I'm only a year older than Anand, so *I'm* young, too. Once when I told my dad how unfair it all is, he said, "Anjali, what's fair is that you get to cook with Deema. Ain't that yuh hobby?" Dad's right — food is my thing. Plus, if I didn't help, it would be really hard on Deema, so I try not to complain.

I finish scrubbing the last colander and rinse it off. I dry my hands, then go to the front of the kitchen and begin helping Deema fill orders. It's dark outside now, and my father turns on the restaurant's CD player. Steel drum music fills the place. Customers tap their feet, drum on the tables, singing about *soca* and island life, wrapping themselves in the rhythms of David Rudder's famous voice. My mom says that when she was pregnant with me and she played a David Rudder CD, I would start moving in her belly. Now the music makes my belly leap with its beat. I dance a little while we fill rotis and put *aloo* pies in the foil containers next to small plastic cups of pepper sauce.

It's hard not to be in a good mood, especially since tomorrow is Saturday, when Deema and I are taking the kids' cooking class at the Institute of Culinary Education in Manhattan. The classes are a gift from Deema. David Rudder's got me moving fast and light on my feet, carrying rotis, *aloo* pies, pepper sauce, and my own rocking *soca* beat to our customers. Deema smiles at me. She's humming softly to the music as she works.

# Aloo Pies

2 cups all-purpose flour

pinch of salt

1/2 cup water

2 teaspoons baking powder

1 pound Yukon gold or other boiling potatoes, boiled and peeled

1/2 teaspoon salt

hot pepper sauce, to taste

1/2 cup canola oil

1 small onion, chopped

5 large cloves garlic, minced

1/2 Roma tomato, seeded and chopped

1. Mix together the flour, pinch of salt, and
baking powder. Add just enough water —
about half a cup — to bring the dough
together, and knead until smooth and elastic, about 5 minutes. Form into balls about

2 inches in diameter, and set aside to rest for 15 minutes.

2. Mash the potatoes, 1/2 teaspoon salt, and hot pepper sauce together and set aside.

3. Heat a large frying pan with 1 tablespoon of the canola oil and fry the onion until it is softened and clear. Add the garlic and fry 30 seconds more. Add the tomato and cook 1 minute longer.

4. Add the mashed potato mixture to the frying pan and mix well so all the ingredients are thoroughly combined. Cook for 1 minute more, and remove from heat. Allow to cool.

5. Flatten a dough ball to about 4 inches in diameter. Place 1 to 2 tablespoons of the potato filling atop a flattened ball and fold it over in a half moon. Using a fork, crimp the edges. Holding the pie in one hand, gently press and flatten it into an oblong shape, roughly 5 inches long, taking care

not to squeeze out the potato filling. Repeat with each dough ball.

6. Heat the remaining oil in a heavy-bottomed frying pan and add the *aloo* pies. Do not crowd the pan. Fry on both sides until golden brown, remove, and drain.

Makes about 15 pies

CHAPTER FOUR

Possibilities

The Institute of Culinary Education takes up five floors in a big office building on Twenty-third Street in Manhattan. From some of the classroom kitchens you can see the Empire State Building ten blocks north. This morning, sunlight flashes off the windows of the high-rise.

The best part of these classes is that I get to touch and smell and cook with ingredients we never use at home or in the roti shop. It's like Christmas and my birthday all rolled into one. If I had one wish — besides being a Food Network star — it would be to win a shopping spree in an expensive grocery store where I could buy anything I wanted.

When I turn away from the window behind the big sinks like the ones we have in the roti shop, I see that today's Kids Cook Tapas class with Chef Nyla is filling up. Deema is already chatting with the father and daughter who are seated at two of the six stations set up at one of the three long stainless steel tables that make a neat row down the center of the room. At the end of the class, the tables will be pushed together and draped with white tablecloths so we can eat everything we prepare.

At the other tables, adults and kids take their places. Some, like Deema, are grandparents, others are parents, and one girl is here with a young woman she calls Auntie. I sit next to Deema and wait.

Chef Nyla Jones comes into the room. Petite, with light brown skin and a mass of blond ringlet curls piled on top of her head, Chef Nyla looks trim and confident in her white chef's jacket with the school's colors, red and gray, piped on the collar. She has two markers and a meat thermometer clipped onto the jacket's lapel. Her sleeves are neatly rolled up. When I'm a real professional, I hope to look just like her.

I've taken a lot of classes with Chef Nyla, and the thing I like best about her is that she always has time for any question, no matter how simple or complicated. She's always willing to teach a special cooking trick or knife skill. During the last class I took with her — one on cake decorating — she asked me what part of India my parents were from, and she seemed genuinely excited to learn that they were actually born in Trinidad.

"That's some of my favorite food in the world," Chef Nyla told me.

Chef Nyla closes the wide glass door to the class-room and stands in front of the class. After waiting a minute for everyone to settle down, she says, "Good morning, class. I'm Chef Nyla Jones. I hope you're all in the mood for a feast of tapas!"

I listen carefully as Chef Nyla describes tapas as many small dishes that are served with wine in Spain.

I take careful notes in the large hardback sketch-book I use for my culinary projects and questions. It's filled with clippings from food magazines and the *New York Times* food section. On the back page I keep all of my usernames and passwords for the food blogs I follow, and on the inside cover I have a running list of cookbooks I want to buy.

I turn to the front of my notebook, where I've sta-pled a piece of card stock on the bottom half of the cover to form a pocket. I pull out the neatly folded piece of paper I put there this morning. It's Deema's Easy Curry Chicken recipe that I've typed on my computer to give Chef Nyla when she makes her way to our table in the back.

Soon it's time to start preparing. I move closer to Deema, who is still talking to the father and daughter and discussing a plan for today's cooking assignment.

Deema introduces me. "Anjali, this is Don and Kerry. They'd like to work as a table team, and I think that's a great idea. We can all get the ingredients together, then let each team take two or three recipes."

Deema explains that she and I work in our roti shop.

"Okay, then," says Don cheerfully, slapping his hands together. "We are all yours, Rosie! Glad to have the guidance!"

Soon we're all busy dashing to the dry goods station at the back of the kitchen, measuring out flour, sugar, salt, and spices into plastic cups and stainless steel bowls. We measure out precise weights of ground shrimp and chicken breast on parchment paper laid across the scale. I place sheets of parchment paper on large sheet trays and use a black Sharpie marker to divide each sheet in half. Next, I write the recipe names on the bottom of each half of the sheet and neatly line up the ingredients for that recipe on top.

"What do you think, Rosie?" Don is saying to Deema. "What if Kerry and I start the empanada filling?"

"Good, good," she answers. "We'll start skewering the chicken and getting the grilling sauce ready."

Over the next two hours we work steadily on our recipes, making mushroom risotto that we form into golf ball–size shapes, tucking pieces of cheese into their middles, then breading and deep-frying them. We make a black-olive tapenade, tiny spinach quiches, and chicken skewers that we grill with peanut *satay* sauce.

The most fun to make are the finger-size empanadas, which are little turnovers stuffed with meat, vegetables, or even fruit as a dessert. Ours are stuffed with shrimp we have ground in the food processor with chili peppers and cilantro and then fried in oil with onions and garlic.

I make the dough as Kerry makes the shrimp. I love the way flour feels on my skin, silky and smooth, how it can change to anything from a gooey paste to hard like a rock. I add salt and swirl the flour around with my fingers, enjoying the feeling, before adding bits of butter, which I squeeze into the dough. Finally, I add ice water, drop by drop, pinching the dough into balls and placing it in the refrigerator to cool down.

While we wait for the dough to chill, we make a dessert of coconut *panna cottas* topped with finely chopped papaya, mango, and passion fruit that has been tossed lightly with a little lime juice.

"Here, let's add this, too," I say, holding the small pile of mint I've chopped. I take in its clean, green aroma before holding my hand up in front of Kerry to smell, too.

"Smells like gum," she says, and laughs. I laugh, too, while I mix the mint into the chopped fruit.

While we work, Don teases my grandmother cheerfully, and she teases him back. I overhear him say he's an investment banker who lives in Manhattan. Kerry is his youngest child — she was born when he was fifty — and he and her mother are divorced.

"Where do you go to school?" asks Kerry. We're cooking the risotto, stirring in chicken stock.

"Forest Hills School. You?" I answer.

"I go to Manhattan Country Day," she says. "Do you like Forest Hills?"

"It's okay. My parents want me to take the Stuyvesant test, though."

Stuyvesant is a special high school for smart kids that is located in downtown Manhattan. You have to take a test to get in and it's free if you do because it's a public school. Thousands of kids from every borough take the test, hoping to get accepted. "You don't seem happy about it," says Kerry.

"It's not that I'm not happy about it, I just really want to go to a school that also has a culinary program, like C-CAP — you know, the Careers through Culinary Arts Program?"

"Really?" says Kerry. She looks surprised. "No offense, I thought those programs were for the, uh, the special ed kids. Or at least those who probably won't go to college. You seem pretty smart, not like them."

I laugh. "Well, thanks," I say, giggling. "I know people think that, and it's partly true, I guess. But a lot of kids who are doing well in school do the program, too. The problem is you have to go to regular public school to get into C-CAP. Forest Hills is private."

"And let me guess, there is no way your parents want you to go to regular public school, right?"

"Right." I sigh. "You got it."

Just then Chef Nyla walks up behind us, placing a hand on each of our shoulders. "Looking good, girls," she says pleasantly. "Just keep on stirring."

"Um, Chef?" I say tentatively as Chef Nyla is turning to go to the next station.

"Yes, Anjali?"

"One second . . ." I hand the spoon to Kerry. "Could you take over for a minute?" Kerry shrugs and takes the spoon.

"I have something for you," I say, moving toward our table. Reaching into my notebook, I pull out the curry chicken recipe.

"This is my grandmother's Easy Curry Chicken recipe. You said you like Trini food." I stop, embarrassed.

Chef Nyla takes the page and scans it with interest.

"Thank you," she says, smiling. "Deema's Easy Curry Chicken. This is great, Anjali! One of my favorite Trinidad dishes, made even more special because it's your grandmother's own recipe. Actually, I have something I want to give you, too. Can you see me after class?"

"Sure. Of course. Yeah."

The class comes to an end all too soon for me, and the groups work together plating their dishes and setting them in the middle of the tables. There is grape juice sangria with orange, nectarine, and apple slices floating on top. The school staff has set out plates and silverware. Everyone takes their places at the table.

We all eat, trying one another's dishes, complimenting on tastes, asking about spices, and chatting about our love of food. Afterward, we divide the leftovers in the takeaway tins the school provides for that purpose. As I pack my bag, I see Don still talking excitedly to Deema. He hands her a card and Deema smiles at him. Chef Nyla comes up to me, holding a piece of paper in her hand.

"Anjali, this is what I wanted you to have," she says. I take the paper and begin to read about a Food Network contest for a new show called *Super Chef Kids*. "I think you could do this," Chef Nyla is saying. "You are a natural cook and you're dedicated. I'd like to see you try out."

I look from the paper to my teacher. My stomach starts to flutter. This is exactly the kind of break I've been dreaming of. "Really?" I say hopefully.

"Yes, *really*, Anjali. I hope you do it," she says, smiling and giving my arm a squeeze. "I wrote down my e-mail address on the paper if you want my help with the essay or the application."

"I'm so excited the only thing I can manage to say is thanks!"

"No problem. I'll talk to you soon," says the chef, beginning to unbutton her jacket and walking out of the room. She stops by Deema and says good-bye, shaking her hand and Don's, then waving to Kerry as she leaves.

I look down again at the paper in my hand. It says there has to be an essay and a short home video as part of the submission. Maybe Linc will help me with that. He got a very good digital video camera for his birthday over the summer. The application says that if they like you, there will be a tryout at the Food Network studios. My heart begins to pound — hard. I read every word of the fine print. The deadline for the application is November 15, only three weeks away. I'll have to ask Linc to help over one of the upcoming weekends. I keep reading, trying to skim it all quickly before Deema calls me to leave.

"Ready, *bayti*?" she says from the doorway.

Looking up at my grandmother, I quickly fold the paper and put it in the pocket of my notebook.

"Yes, Deema, I'm coming."

Deema's Easy Curry Chicken

4 boneless chicken breasts, cut into
1/2-inch cubes

3 tablespoons chopped onion

2 cloves garlic, chopped

1 1/2 teaspoons chopped fresh *shado beni* or
cilantro

1 teaspoon ground cumin

3 tablespoons Trinidad curry powder

2 tablespoons canola oil

3/4 cup chicken stock

1 medium Yukon gold potato, peeled and
cut into 1/2-inch cubes

1/2 teaspoon salt

1/2 cup coconut milk

1. Make the marinade: In a medium bowl,
mix the onion, garlic, *shado beni* or cilantro,
cumin, and 2 teaspoons of the curry powder. Coat the chicken in the marinade and

set aside for at least 20 minutes but preferably overnight in the refrigerator.

2. Heat the oil in a deep saucepan and
add the marinated chicken cubes. Add the
remaining curry powder and mix well.
Sauté for 2 to 3 minutes.

3. Add the chicken stock, potatoes, and
salt. Simmer for 15 minutes and continue
to cook until the sauce thickens, about 5
minutes more.

4. Add the coconut milk and simmer for 3
minutes more. Taste and adjust the season-
ings as desired. Serve with rice or rotis.

Makes 4 servings

CHAPTER FIVE

Decisions

Where r u? All rdy, I text on the hand-me-down Nokia phone my father gave me. I hate this phone. It's a free-bie that came with the calling plan, and it's so old that the numbers and letters are almost rubbed off. Linc has an iPhone, and most of the other kids at school have an iPhone or BlackBerry or some other smart-phone. When I'm with them, I try to never take out my cell unless I absolutely have to, to answer a call from my parents.

At ʃ'way, comes Linc's reply. That's good. It means he's just gotten off the bus at the subway station at Liberty.

For my TV audition video, I'm planning to make my famous Coconut Dark Chocolate Chip Cookies, which I spike with coconut flakes and gourmet chocolate made from cocoa beans from Trinidad if I can get it. It's expensive and cuts into my allowance savings, but for something like this it's worth it. Besides, they're Linc's favorite cookies and it will be a nice gift for his help.

"Anj?" Linc's voice comes through our kitchen window. He's yelling up from the front sidewalk. I run down the stairs and let him in.

"What's going on?" he says as he steps over the threshold.

"Everything is ready," I say, locking the dead bolt behind him.

"Cool," he answers, taking the steps two at a time. When we reach the kitchen, Linc pulls the iPod earbuds out of his ears and neatly wraps them around his iPhone. Next, he pulls out a video camera that's small enough to fit in the palm of his hand.

"That's it?" I say doubtfully.

"Yep, that's it," says Linc, smiling. "It's small but mighty. Great digital quality."

I shrug. I'll have to take Linc's word for it. He's the gadget geek, not me.

"Okay, so I figure we'll just start with an intro about me and then I'll start making the cookies," I say. "I've been rehearsing."

"Don't worry, we can do multiple takes," Linc says. "I'm going to edit the video on my Mac and even add a little intro music. Maybe some steel pan drums. Or I found this song called 'Kuchela.'"

"Really? 'Kuchela'?"

Kuchela is a condiment made from hot peppers and grated green mangoes. It's spicy and tangy and delicious to eat with curry, but it's hard to think someone could write a song about it.

"Yeah, really," he says, turning on the camera and slowly panning it over the bowls and the stand mixer, one of my prized purchases I bought with allowance and Christmas money saved up over two years. "Just leave the filming to me," Linc says.

I take my place behind the counter and try to look serious and professional. Linc puts the camera down. "Anj, you have to smile. Look happy. Who's going to want to watch a pissy-looking cook?"

"I'm not pissy looking," I snap. "I'm just waiting for you to say start."

"Okay then . . . action!"

Trying hard not to roll my eyes, I stretch my mouth in what I hope will seem like a big, happy, not too fake smile.

"Hi, I'm Anjali Krishnan, and I'm from Richmond

Hill, Queens — or as some people call it, Little Trinidad — here in New York City. I'm in eighth grade at the Forest Hills School. Cooking is my most favorite hobby. Today I'm going to make an old favorite with a new twist, Coconut Dark Chocolate Chip Cookies. The great thing about these cookies is that there's something for every kid to do while making them, so no one has to be left out."

Linc gives me a thumbs-up sign from behind the camera. I reach toward the butter and drop it in the mixer. I pick up the brown sugar and add that, too.

"Cut! Cut!" yells Linc, making me jump.

"What? What is it?"

"You have to tell us what you're doing!" he says. "Think about all the Food Network chefs — they say *what* they're doing while they're doing it."

"Oh! Okay," I say. "Good point. But you don't have to yell. This isn't a movie set." I look down at the butter and sugar in the bowl and frown.

"I don't have any more butter and sugar," I say. "What do I do?"

Linc puts down the camera and considers this for a minute. "Well, how about I film you walking over to the mixer and saying something like 'I already have the butter and sugar in the bowl to start the cookies.' Oh, and say the amounts. They always say the amounts."

I nod and walk back toward the end of the counter.

"And . . . action!" yells Linc, making me jump again.

I walk toward the mixer, put my hand on the switch, and say, "I already have two sticks of softened, unsalted butter and three-quarters of a cup of brown sugar in the bowl." I reach across to another bowl on the counter and begin to pour from that. "Now I'm adding three-quarters of a cup of white sugar. We'll blend all of this on medium speed until light and fluffy — about four minutes."

Linc gives me the thumbs-up and again puts the camera down. "I'm going to do a close-up of the bowl, then start filming you in the last thirty seconds of mixing. No one wants to watch a mixing bowl churning away for four minutes."

I nod and step aside so he can get a good view into the mixer. For the next half an hour we keep filming, with me adding ingredients and then pausing while they mix. Sometimes I flub the words and have to start again. I glance at the clock. Forty-five minutes have passed. We only have a little over another hour to get this done. With all this stopping and starting we'll need every minute of it. I thought this whole thing would take only twenty minutes, the time it takes to mix up the cookie dough. I didn't figure on how many times you'd have to do something to get it right on film.

Finally, it's time to spoon the dough onto cookie sheets that I've already prepared. After I put them in the oven, Linc plops down at the kitchen table while I clean up the mixing bowls and measuring spoons.

"Are you sure you can edit all those pieces into a real video?" I say.

"Yes, Anj, don't worry. I'll finish it up over the weekend and bring a disc to school on Monday. Then we'll mail it at lunchtime, okay?"

"Yeah, cool," I say anxiously. "Thanks, Linc, I really appreciate it."

"No problem," he says, smiling. "Let's finish up."

"Okay, we just have to wait for the timer to go off," I tell Linc.

Once the digital display on the stove reaches ten, Linc focuses the camera on it while it counts down the seconds to zero. He motions over to me to take out the cookies. I place them on the counter to cool.

"You'll want to let the cookies cool for about five minutes before you take them off the cookie sheet," I say to the camera.

"Almost there, Anj," says Linc, turning off the camera and reaching for a cookie. He pulls back his hand, shaking and blowing on his fingers.

"Didn't I just say cooling takes five minutes?"

"That's for the folks in TV land," Linc says. "Not the producer!" Reaching forward again, he grabs a cookie and tosses it from hand to hand to cool it off before popping the whole thing in his mouth.

After five minutes, I use a spatula to carefully take the cookies off the cookie sheet and place them on one of my mother's special china plates that I've taken from the dining room cabinet. I put it down on the table between me and Linc and pour two tall glasses of sorrel, a hibiscus drink that Deema makes every week.

"Ready when you are," I tell Linc.

Linc stands and switches on the camera.

"Okay, action!" he mumbles around a mouthful of cookie.

"Here are the finished cookies, hot from the oven," I say to the camera. I pick one up from the plate and break it in half. The gooey molten chocolate oozes out over my fingers. "You can see the pieces of melted chocolate and coconut inside." I take a bite and swallow. "Delicious! Especially with a tall, cool glass of sorrel." I pick up the glass and take a sip. "But for that recipe, you'll have to tune in next time! Thanks for watching!" I continue to smile brightly at the camera, trying not to blink, until Linc says, "Cut!"

I let out a deep breath and slump in my chair. "Wow, that was a lot harder than I thought!"

"Yep, but it will be great!" Linc puts the camera away in his backpack, then hoists the pack onto his shoulder. He heads for the stairs.

"One sec — you take the cookies home," I say, rushing to grab a plastic bag.

"Hey! Cool! Thanks!"

"Least I could do."

I finish cleaning up. They'll be expecting me down at the restaurant pretty soon.

Weeks pass with no letter from the Food Network.

Thanksgiving comes and goes. On the day before Christmas vacation, there's still no letter from the Food Network.

Will they *ever* call me? I felt so sure the video was good — and Linc felt even surer. But now, all I can picture is the people at the Food Network looking at my video and laughing.

I slide into the cafeteria seat next to Linc and reach into my knapsack for my lunch: leftovers from last night's pilau, a rice and bean dish with chicken and pieces of pumpkin.

"Any word?" Linc says.

"Not yet," I answer, unwrapping the plastic fork and knife from the paper napkin and beginning to eat. The chicken is so tender it's practically in shreds. The rice is fluffy but not sticky. The whole thing is good and spicy. I have to drink a lot of water while I eat it. But it's comfort food. Real good.

"Oh, well," I say. I'm trying to be cool, show that it doesn't bother me. "We tried. I guess it wasn't good enough."

Linc puts down his sandwich. "You're not fooling me, Anj," he says. "Just hang tight — you never know."

That night and the next day are busy ones at the roti shop, and we close late on Christmas Eve. It's midnight by the time we drag ourselves home.

On the way back to our house, Dad and I walk in the cold darkness of December. "Anjali," he says, "have you been preparing for the Stuyvesant exam? It's coming up."

I'm quiet, thinking. "I know" is all I can manage. Then, "Yeah, I've been getting ready."

Okay, so I'm lying. But I've been thinking about the Stuyvesant test, which is a way of getting ready. Sort of.

Deema and I wake up early on Christmas to get the family's big Christmas lunch together while also making breakfast. After everyone gets up and shares presents, my mom sits at the dining table to study while Dad relaxes on the couch to read his new book. Anand plays a new video game. Deema and I go back to the kitchen to work.

"*Bayti*, is something troubling you?" Deema asks while we chop vegetables.

"No, Deema, why?" I answer. I'm able to avoid my grandmother's eyes by checking on the pot of bubbling sorrel drink.

"You seem like your mind somewhere else," she says.

"I have a school project on my mind is all." I don't want to talk about the video audition, not even with Deema.

For the rest of the holiday break, I keep worrying about the letter, rushing to the mailbox as soon as the postman comes or dashing up the stairs to go through the pile on the table if he gets there when I'm not home. Things are slow at the restaurant after Christmas and I finish all of my schoolwork in the first few days off. So I use the time left to study for the Stuyvesant exam, which is coming up in January.

I've got a few more weeks to study. I'm restless at night, not really sleeping, thinking about C-CAP, the Food Network, and our roti shop — and I'm rolling new recipes around in my thoughts, inventing them as I lie in bed, tossing.

By the time I go back to school after the New Year, I figure I definitely haven't made the Food Network cut and try to put the whole thing out of my mind.

"Now I just feel stupid," I say to Linc at school. "Like they probably watched my video and cracked up all day long."

"Come on, Anjali, that's dumb," says Linc. "The video was good."

"Yeah, I know," I answer miserably. "I guess maybe *I* wasn't good enough."

That afternoon I go straight to the restaurant from school, doing my homework at an empty table when things are quiet and studying hard in the final stretch before the Stuyvesant exam. By the time I get home I'm almost too tired to stop in the kitchen for a glass of water. I sit down at the kitchen table with my drink and leaf through the pile of mail there. I almost miss my name on one of the envelopes. I don't recognize the return address so I assume it's for one of my parents or Deema. SCRIPPS NETWORKS it says in big letters, and underneath: Food Network.

I snatch up the letter and tear open the envelope. I stop for a moment before pulling out the paper.

Dear Ms. Krishnan,
> *Thank you for your recent video contribution to the* Super Chef Kids *contest.*

I close my eyes for a few seconds. I breathe. This sounds like a kiss-off. I open my eyes. I slowly keep reading.

> *We are pleased to say you have been chosen as one of the finalists to come to the Food Network studios, accompanied by a parent or guardian, for a live tryout.*

I leap up. I'm dancing quietly, feeling the rhythms of David Rudder fill me. I want to yell but glance quickly at the clock. It's too late to call Linc. I sit down and bounce in my seat while I read about the details of the Food Network audition.

The tryout is on January 20. The same day as the Stuyvesant entrance exam. That's when David Rudder's *soca* beat stops suddenly. And I'm breathing even more now — actually, I'm trying to breathe.

 # Coconut Dark Chocolate Chip Cookies

1 cup (two sticks) unsalted butter

3/4 cup white sugar

3/4 cup packed brown sugar

1 large egg

1 teaspoon vanilla

2 1/4 cups all-purpose flour

1 teaspoon baking soda

1/2 teaspoon salt

2 cups semisweet chocolate chips or 10 ounces good-quality dark chocolate chopped into chip-size pieces

1 cup sweetened coconut flakes

1. Preheat oven to 375 degrees Fahrenheit. Place the rack in the middle position in the oven.

2. Combine the butter and sugars in the bowl of a standing mixer. Mix on medium-

high until light and fluffy, about four minutes.

3. Add the egg and vanilla and mix well, stopping to scrape down the bowl as necessary.

4. Stir in the flour, baking soda, and salt until well combined.

5. Stir in the chocolate chips or chocolate pieces and coconut flakes. Mix well to form a stiff dough.

6. Drop the dough by rounded tablespoonfuls 2 inches apart onto ungreased cookie sheets that have been lined with parchment paper. Bake 8 to 10 minutes or until light brown. The centers will be soft. Let cool for 5 minutes, then remove from the cookie sheets and place on wire racks to finish cooling.

Makes 3 dozen cookies

 # Sorrel Drink

8 cups water

1 cinnamon stick

6 cloves

1/2 cup dried sorrel flowers (available in Caribbean markets) or 4 hibiscus tea bags

2 cups sugar

1. Place 8 cups of water, the cinnamon stick, and the cloves in a saucepan and bring to a boil. Add the sorrel or the hibiscus tea bags and sugar. Simmer for 2 minutes.

2. Remove the mixture from the heat; cover and steep at least one hour but preferably overnight.

3. Strain the sorrel through a fine-mesh sieve or remove tea bags and store in

glass bottles in the refrigerator. Serve chilled. Sorrel keeps for up to 1 week.

Makes 6 to 8 servings

PART

TWO

Ambition

Recipe for Ambition

4 parts desire

1 part hope

5 dashes moxie

3 cups plans, well laid

1. Pour the desire into a heavy pot placed over high heat. Allow it to come to a hard boil and add the hope. Stir well and lower heat to a simmer.

2. When the mixture begins to thicken, add the moxie and mix rapidly, using a whisk. Remove from the heat.

3. Allow the mixture to cool until it is no longer steaming but still hot to the touch. Carefully fold in the well-laid plans until completely combined.

4. Pour into a heavy ceramic dish and allow to gel.

CHAPTER SIX

Ambition

"Deema?" We're drying dishes.

"Yes, *bayti*?"

"I want to talk to Mom and Dad about something."

"What *something*?"

I tell her about making the finals and the fact that the actual tryout is the same day as the Stuyvesant test. The words fly out of me like butterflies eager to escape a jar. When I'm done, Deema is quiet, still drying the dishes.

"Deema?"

She puts down the plate in her hand and gives me a small smile.

"Your parents aren't going to agree to that, Anjali," she says. "I'm not so sure it's a good idea myself."

"But —" I begin.

Deema holds up one hand.

"This is sudden, *bayti*, and I'm not sure how I feel about it. I can't agree to something I'm not sure is right."

My heart starts to pound slowly but hard. I need Deema's help. She's the only one who can reason with my dad. My mom usually goes along with what he wants. I sigh and put the last dish away, then take off my apron. I look at Deema, who nods, taking off her own apron. She gestures toward the living room. Her little smile tells me she's going to help smooth things over somehow.

In the living room, my father is parked in front of the TV. He's watching a soccer game with Anand. Mom's reading one of her textbooks at the table. I sit on the couch arm, waiting for the game to be over. It'll be a lot worse if I interrupt my dad's game. Deema joins my mother at the table and leafs through a catalog that's come in the newspaper.

The game finally ends.

"Dad? Can I talk to you and Mom about something?"

"Sure, what's up?" he says, turning toward me. I stand nervously and reach into my pocket, pulling out the acceptance letter for the Food Network tryout. I hand it to him silently. My mother looks up from her textbook while Dad reads.

"What is it, Anjali?" she asks.

Before I can respond, my father answers. There's a big smile on his face.

"Could you believe it, Lottie? The girl actually got a shot at that Food Network thing."

Anand looks away from the TV toward me. "No kidding, sis? WOW!" he says, getting up to give me a high five.

"Sweetheart, that's wonderful!" my mom says, and rushes over to hug me.

I feel dizzy, like when I'm racing around the restaurant kitchen in the heat and I haven't had enough water. Deema sits quietly at the table, still looking at the catalog.

"Ma? You hearin' this?" my father calls over to her. "Ma?"

Deema stands up. "Yes, son, I hearin', but I think Anjie has something else to say."

I nod and try to swallow. My mouth is completely dry and I'm finding it hard to talk.

"Well, you see, the tryout day is the same day as the Stuyvesant test," I begin.

"Well, you can go after!" Dad booms.

"I wish. But it's the same time, Dad," I say miserably.

My mom puts her arm around my shoulders.

"Ah, that's too bad," he says. "But at least you know you made it. That's an achievement. Next time, then."

"Dad, that's what I wanted to talk to you about," I say, speaking quickly before he can interrupt me. "I'd like to do this instead. It's a once in a lifetime chance — I might even get my own show! Plus, I can take the Stuyvesant test next year."

Mom interrupts. "Where do you propose to go to school, then, Anjali? You know that even with the scholarship, Forest Hills School is expensive for us. Even on the one in a million chance you win this thing and get your own show, you'll still have to go to school."

"I can go to high school here in Queens," I say. "It's free, and there is the C-CAP program I told you about."

"Absolutely not," my father breaks in. "This is foolishness. You are taking the Stuyvesant test. Period."

"But, Dad, that's not a sure thing, either. I might not get in!"

"Rubbish, Anjali," he says firmly. "You are one of the smartest kids in your school. Of course you're getting in."

"Please, Dad —"

"No, the conversation is over," he says. "Be happy you made the tryout and drop it. This cooking on TV is not your future."

"Why?" I say angrily. "*Cooking* is our family business. It's *your* future!"

"Anjali," my father says, raising his voice. "Do *not* test my patience. Cooking is a *hobby* for you. That's it — a hobby! Do you think I like standing up in a roti shop all day? It's not my future by choice, it's my future by necessity. I want more for you and Anand. You are too young to know what's good for you. That is my decision to make."

"But, Dad —"

"No, Anjali!" he yells, making me jump.

My mother is looking at the floor. She still has her arm around my shoulders.

"Mom?" I whisper. She shakes her head slightly.

"Deema?"

"Your father knows what's best for you, *bayti*," Deema answers softly.

I pull away from my mother and look angrily at them all. Anand has his arms crossed and is slumped on the couch. He won't look at me. This is worse than having a bucket of ice thrown on my head.

"I don't even want to go to stupid Stuyvesant! Do any of you even care about that?"

I run to my room and slam the door as hard as I can. I want to break something, to keep screaming, but I know my father would have no problem giving me a smack if I did that. I sit at my desk and stare out the window at the traffic on the Van Wyck Expressway.

There has to be another way. And I'm going to find it.

I sit on the wooden bench and unlace my skates. It's Saturday. Linc and I are spending the morning at the ice rink at the World's Fair grounds in Flushing, a few neighborhoods away.

"Anj, it's too cold to sit out here," says Linc. "Why can't we talk inside the skate rental hall?"

"It's too noisy in there."

Linc blows into his hands, then shoves them into his pockets.

"I made the Food Network finals," I blurt out.

Linc pulls his right hand out of his pocket. He slaps the air between us for a high five. *"Pow!"*

But before Linc can get too happy, I tell him. "The callback is the same day as the Stuyvesant test."

Linc puts his hand down. "Aw, crap," he says. "The same time, too?"

I nod miserably.

"Maybe you can get a special pass or something. They can let you take the test another time," he says. "You know — a dis — what's that word?"

"A dispensation?" I say. "Not likely. My parents would have to agree and they've already said no."

Linc hunches into the collar of his coat. "That just sucks," he mumbles from behind the puffy cloth.

"Linc . . ." I begin. He cuts his eyes at me. He knows I've already got a plan that involves him. "That's why I need your help," I say softly.

He's squirming like I'm about to give him a shot. I can only just see Linc's eyes over the collar of his coat.

"How do you mean?"

"I'm not taking the Stuyvesant test," I say firmly. "I *can't* take it."

Linc shakes his head. "I'm not gonna have this conversation with you. I don't like where it's going."

"Please, Linc. Please listen," I say, tugging at the edge of his jacket. "Just hear me out."

Linc flings himself onto a bench. He's listening.

"Linc, this means everything to me, even if I have to get in trouble and make my parents angry. If I make the TV show, Mom and Dad won't stay mad. You should have seen how happy they were about the audition before they found out it's the same day as the Stuyvesant test." I'm talking faster before Linc can get a word in. "Imagine me on a TV show! Plus, there's no guarantee I would even get in to Stuyvesant."

Linc looks at me and sticks his fist in the air between us. "First," he says, sticking out his thumb, "your parents will stay mad. Second" — he sticks out his forefinger — "they won't think any TV show is as important as school, and third — of course you'll get in to Stuyvesant."

I take a deep breath.

"Linc, I am going to do it one way or the other. All I'm asking is that you help me a little. I won't get you in trouble or anything. I just want you to take the Stuyvesant test, then tell me what was on the test after you take it, in case anyone asks me about it. Simple."

Linc is quiet.

"Okay, Anjali, even if I do, don't you have to have a parent or someone with you at the Food Network audition?" he asks. "How you gonna get around that?"

"I'll think of something."

That night, awake in bed, I do think of cooking. Quietly, I go to our kitchen, where there are always dry coconuts, ready for grating. So I grate. And I think of sweet bread. That's when something else sweet comes to me — an idea for who can go with me to the Food Network audition as my "parent."

Coconut Sweet Bread

3 cups flour

1 cup sugar

1 tablespoon baking powder

1 teaspoon salt

2 cups finely grated fresh coconut

1/3 cup raisins (optional)

1 large egg, beaten

1/2 cup evaporated milk

1/2 cup fresh coconut water

1 teaspoon mixed essence or vanilla

1 cup (2 sticks) unsalted butter, melted and cooled

1/2 teaspoon coconut essence

granulated sugar for dusting

1. Preheat oven to 350 degrees Fahrenheit. Grease and flour two 9-inch loaf pans.

2. Sift the flour, sugar, baking powder, and

salt together, and stir in the coconut and raisins, if using.

3. In a separate bowl, combine the egg, milk, coconut water, mixed essence or vanilla, butter, and coconut essence.

4. Add the liquid ingredients to the dry ones, mixing lightly but thoroughly so all the ingredients are combined.

5. Pour the batter into the loaf pans, filling them two-thirds full.

6. Sprinkle the top of the batter with granulated sugar and bake for about 55 minutes or until a toothpick inserted into the center comes out clean.

Makes 2 loaves

CHAPTER SEVEN

Competition

I braid my ponytail to keep stray hair out of my face during the tryout. My black T-shirt says "Island Spice Roti Shop" on the front. I tuck sneakers into my knapsack along with the small *tawa* Deema bought me a few years back when I was first learning how to make rotis. It's no bigger than a smallish dinner plate, but it will be good for making the little rotis I'm going to use for my main dish at the audition.

Our house is so quiet. Everyone left for the day. They think I'm on my way to take the test at Stuyvesant, but the only kid I know who's headed to that exam is Linc. I'm taking the A train to the Food Network studios. I open my umbrella against the sleet that is still coming down. It's gathered along the curbs, a dirty gray mess I need to leap over when I cross the street. My heavy backpack bangs against my hip each time I jump.

The train is packed with workers headed into the city for the 8 A.M. work shift. Even though it's so cold outside, all the bodies packed together make the car way hot. I stand between a fat lady in a fuzzy coat and a tall man in a suit. There are so many people I can't get near a pole to hold on to, but together we all make a human wall. There's nowhere to fall even if I lose my footing. I hold my backpack's loop in my right hand, letting it rest on top of my foot. It's so heavy it pulls me down, anchors me in place. My shoulder begins to throb.

Forty minutes later the subway pulls into my stop. The constant flow of passengers in and out of the train means I never did get a seat, and now my right shoulder is killing me. When I get to the top of the subway stairs at Fourteenth Street and Eighth Avenue, it's at least stopped sleeting. I walk through the streets a few more blocks toward Chelsea Market, where the Food Network studios are located.

Inside Chelsea Market I walk along the snaking black hallway toward the middle of the complex to the café, where my "parent" is waiting to accompany me to the audition. She's wearing jeans and a bright red V-neck sweater. Her blond ringlets frame her face.

It's the first time I've seen her in street clothes. She looks so young and cool.

"Hey, Anjali!" she says, smiling. "You ready?"

I'm glad to see her. "Ready, Chef Nyla," I say.

"Today I'm just Nyla," she says. "Your friend Nyla."

I smile and feel my body relax.

"Let's go, Nyla."

I hoist my ten-ton knapsack over my shoulder. Nyla knows her way around this place. I'm right on her heels, following closely. We ride the elevator to the sixth floor.

There's a young guy sitting behind a tall oval desk and a few kids sitting on the funky modern couches with their parents.

Nyla walks up to the desk and signs us in, then comes to stand beside me. All the chairs are full.

"They said the associate producer will be out to take us to the greenroom shortly," she tells me.

Ten minutes later, a heavyset woman with cornrows comes out and introduces herself.

"Hey, everybody." She smiles. "I'm Paula, and I'm gonna take you all back to the greenroom. You'll have a little makeup and then the producer will come out and tell you how it's gonna go."

All of the kids and their adults file after Paula into a door that leads to a bunch of cubicles, then through a back hallway that looks like it belongs in a warehouse. We finally get to an empty room with some couches and two chairs like you see at the hairdresser. The room is tiny.

"Here you go. It'll be a little tight, but make yourselves comfortable," says Paula.

Nyla grabs my hand and heads quickly to the couch, plopping us down abruptly to make sure we have a place to sit. The other contestants — a girl with red hair and a nose ring, an African American boy, and a blond girl with thick glasses and a sharp pageboy haircut — and their parents stand awkwardly in the center of the room or lean on the wall.

A woman with curly blond hair and square purple glasses comes in. She's wearing a long skirt that looks like a bunch of fabric patches sewn together. The heels on her black leather boots are spiky. She's also wearing a barely noticeable headset in her ear and holding a little black box in her hand.

"Hi, folks, I'm Brenda Wokowski, the executive producer of *Super Chef Kids*." This lady is all business, no smiles. "Here's the breakdown of what will happen today. We're going to split up into groups of three contestants. The first are" — she looks down at the clipboard she's carrying and my throat goes tight — "Anjali Krishnan, He Kyong Park, and Jimmy DeFazio."

I'm up first.

Brenda looks around the room as I step forward along with a heavy kid in a Mets jersey and a slender Asian girl.

"Good," Brenda says, looking each of us over. "A makeup artist will be coming in here in a second, just to give you a little touch-up for the camera. Nothing fancy. Please tell her if there is anything you're allergic to." She pauses again and looks at me and the other girl. "You're okay," she says, pointing at me. "You'll have to put your hair back," she says to He Kyong.

"After that we'll take you into the studio and show you your stations," she finishes. "I'll see you in a little bit — good luck, guys."

After Brenda leaves the room, we all just stand there, not really sure of what to do next. He Kyong goes back and sits in the cosmetic chair. Her mother begins to fuss with her hair.

The makeup artist hustles in a few minutes later. He is a young Latino guy with spiky blond hair and a nose ring. He's also got a headset and a little black box clipped to his black jeans.

"Who's first?" he says in a singsong voice.

Since He Kyong is already at the mirror she goes first, followed by me, then Jimmy. I pull off my jacket and sit down in the chair after He Kyong gets up.

"Hmmm," says the makeup artist, whose name is Abelardo. He tilts my chin up with his fingers and looks at my face from different sides. "You have good skin tone, I won't have to do much." Abelardo works for a few minutes applying makeup with a sponge to the corners of my mouth and on my upper lip, then uses a big brush to dust my whole face with a powder that he tells me matches my skin tone.

"Fabulous," he says, putting a little gloss on my lips. "Try not to bite your lips."

I nod and stare at myself in the mirror. Whoa. I'm surprised to see that I actually look pretty good.

When I come back to the couch, Nyla says, "Beautiful, Anjali."

Brenda comes back just as Abelardo finishes making up Jimmy, who then mashes a Mets cap backward on top of his head. Along with our parents, we file after Brenda through more hallways and into a large kitchen with five parallel counters, each with a cooktop, drawers, and lots of utensils.

People dressed in black chef's jackets embroidered with the Food Network logo dash around.

"New blood, Brenda?" a man calls out, smiling, as we walk past.

"You know it, Chef Rob!" she laughs back. She tells us, "That's Rob. He's the head chef of the test kitchens."

Ahead of us a canvas curtain blocks the rest of the space. When we follow Brenda around it we see that, from the other side, it's a backdrop of the city to make it appear as if we're looking out of the window of a high-rise. The "window" is part of a false wall that makes up one side of the large kitchen where we're going to cook.

Three identical workstations are lined up side by side. Behind each one, an oven in pink, blue, or avocado green is built into the wall. The opposite walls have school lockers and chalkboards. I guess the space is supposed to look like a schoolroom, but it's not like any school I've ever seen.

"Where do they film *Power Chef*?" asks Jimmy as we walk into the space.

"Right here," says Brenda. "This whole studio is taken down and reassembled for each show. We film a series over the course of days or weeks and we store the sets in crates until we need them. You see them weekly, but they are really filmed over just a few days, a long time before."

"Wow," says Jimmy, looking around.

Just then a plump woman with curly shoulder-length black hair walks by.

"Hey! Sam!" Nyla touches the woman's arm.

I recognize her right away. She's Sam Vitelli, one of the Food Network stars and a judge on a lot of the cooking contest shows.

Sam looks pleased to see Nyla. "Nyla," she says. "How you doing, woman? What brings you here?" Nyla and Sam hug each other.

Nyla puts her arm around me. "I'm here with my student who is one of the *Super Chef Kids* finalists," she says proudly. "Anjali, this is —"

"Sam Vitelli," I blurt. I'm totally gushing inside. If I die right now, I will be happy.

Sam's checking me out. "I'm one of the judges," she tells Nyla. "And I see they have our judges' table set up! I'll catch you later!"

"How do you know *her*?" I whisper.

Nyla says, "Believe it or not, we went to high school together. Her dad is a big-time publicity agent for restaurants and chefs and he got her this gig."

I'm still ready to fall over from meeting Sam when Brenda comes in.

"Okay, folks, here we are," she says. "This is Alfie. He's going to walk you through what will happen on the set, and Roger here will mic you guys. The judges will be sitting in that corner." She points to the long table where Sam Vitelli has parked herself next to a slender woman who looks like a model, and a kid a few years older than me.

"Hey, judges, stand up for a second," Alfie calls out, and they all get up. Now that I can see them better, I realize the lady who looks like a model is Daisy Martinez, another Food Network chef and one of my heroes.

"Not that any of these folks need an introduction," Alfie calls out cheerfully, "but allow me to formally acquaint you." He pauses to laugh at his own dumb sense of humor.

"We have Sam Vitelli, star of *The Culinary Tower*. Sam — give a wave," he says.

"Our next judge is another one of our most popular stars, Daisy Martinez," he continues as Daisy smiles big. "And a very special guest, Connor Sebastian, from the Sebastian Boys!"

Connor gives us a small finger wave, then slumps back in his chair.

"Thanks, judges!" Alfie calls out, then turns back to us. "Parents, you can have a seat over there." He points to some folding chairs set up on the other side of the set from the judges. Nyla gives me a thumbs-up.

When Brenda comes by to make sure everything's okay, she does a double take and stares hard at me like she never saw me before.

"What's that on your shirt?" she says.

"What?" I say, looking down.

"That writing," says Brenda. "What does your shirt say?"

I smile proudly. "That's my family's roti shop — Island Spice."

"You can't wear that," Brenda answers flatly. "You can't wear a shirt that has advertising. It will look like the network is giving you free advertising or an endorsement. Do you have another shirt with you?"

Why would I have another shirt? I shake my head.

A production assistant runs up with a bag. "Who needs the T-shirt?" she calls out. I raise my hand.

"Here you go." She tosses the shirt to me.

I go into the ladies' room and find a stall. I unclip the microphone, letting it hang down while I take off my Island Spice shirt. The new T-shirt is bright yellow — my absolute worst color. And it's so big that I look like I'm wearing my father's clothes.

I think of Dad then, and Deema, and how I'm letting down my family *and* lying to them. I start to cry at how much I want all of this — and how much they *don't* want it. Then I remember my TV makeup. *Don't cry,* I tell myself. I tuck the oversize shirt into my pants as best I can. The short sleeves reach my elbows. Pulling the microphone wire up through the neck, I clip it to the collar and step out of the stall. When I get back to the group, Alfie is barking orders.

"Okay, kids, listen up." Alfie's clapping to get our attention. "Each one of you will have your own cooking station. The pullout refrigerators under the counter have all the perishables you'll need to cook your dishes. The drawers have dry goods. The drawers on the side here have utensils and knives." He points to a shelf just under the stove, where there are pots, pans, and mixing bowls. "You'll notice there is a food processor and stand mixer on the counter. We've thought of everything you'll need to cook your dishes."

I try to concentrate on what Alfie's saying. I should be excited to use all of this new equipment, but I still feel crappy and embarrassed about the T-shirt — and upset about going behind my family's back.

"After you cook your own dish, we're going to unveil a market basket," Alfie is saying. "This is a tray of ingredients from which you have to create a dish on the spot. You can use any of the staples in your cupboards or anything left over from your own specialties, but you have to use all the items in the market basket."

I hadn't expected the market basket. *Breathe,* I tell myself, *just breathe.*

"How long will we have?" He Kyong wants to know.

"Half an hour for your dish, and half an hour for the market basket," says Alfie. "There will be a fifteen-minute break after we unveil the market basket so you can use the bathroom, get some water, and think about what you want to do with those ingredients. Everyone clear?" He looks at the three of us. We all nod. "We'll be getting started in a few minutes."

I mentally go through the order of preparation for what I'll be making — my shrimp burgers. I'll have to make the roti dough first. While it rests, I'll make the shrimp paste, then do the jicama slaw. It shouldn't be too hard. I'm worried about that market basket, though — what if it's something I can't work with, like beef or pork?

The start signal has been given.

Quade Jerome, one of the Food Network's emcee personalities, is running around the studio, weaving between the cooking stations like a basketball star on the court.

"So, tell us where you're from, Anjali."

"Richmond Hill," I answer, not looking up from the shrimp I'm trying to quickly peel and throw into the food processor with the pureed green seasoning.

Quade flicks a switch on the microphone with his thumb and leans in a little. "Come on, little sis, you gotta give me more than that," he says pleasantly. He's a light-skinned black man with green eyes. "Look at me and smile, show the camera some love!"

He switches the microphone back on. "For our

non–New York viewers, tell us about Richmond Hill, Anjali!"

I try to smile, though he is really annoying me. "It's in Queens. There are a lot of Indo-Caribbeans there, like my family."

"Keep on cooking!"

I jump and go back to the shrimp.

"Are you making an Indo-Caribbean treat for us today?"

It's hard to cook and talk. I nod. "Um, well, yeah, we eat rotis like I'm going to make for my shrimp burger," I say, glancing nervously from my shrimp to Quade. "You can see the dough over there." I nod over my shoulder to the roti dough on the counter. The cameraman pans to my dough ball. "And we curry just about everything."

"Great! Can't wait to try it — if the judges leave anything!" Quade says.

Quade runs over to Jimmy next and asks what he's cooking.

"These are my grandma's famous smothered Italian pork chops," he says, smiling at the camera. "I'm from

Bensonhurst — that's in Brooklyn. And it's Italian country! *Mangia!*" Jimmy leans toward the camera, one hand on the spoon and stirring tomatoes in a fry pan. He's all showbiz.

I try not to pay attention as Quade runs over to He Kyong, who knows how to smile at the camera. Quade doesn't even have to ask her what she's cooking. She just starts talking.

"I'm making a simple five-mushroom salad that I'll nestle on a bed of rice noodles," she says sweetly to the camera lens. "It doesn't take a lot of effort but it tastes like a million bucks!"

I roll my eyes. *What does a million bucks taste like?*

Next, I make the jicama slaw. I look around the kitchen for a grater but I don't see one here. Opening some drawers, I notice a shredder attachment for the food processor. It means I'll have to wash the bowl.

Dashing over to the processor, I twist the bowl off the base and head to the sink to rinse it out. This takes up time I don't have. I run back, wiping the bowl with my side towel as I go. That's when I notice a spare bowl sitting on the counter a little ways away. This is the bowl I should have used.

I can feel my face getting hot and I'm hoping against hope that no one noticed my silly mistake — but, ugh, here's that pest Quade at my station.

"Feeling leisurely, huh, Anjali?" he says cheerfully. "I see you have time to wash dishes!"

"Maybe she's just not used to a real professional kitchen, Quade!" He Kyong calls out. The camera pans back to her. She bats her eyelashes and winks at the viewers.

What a piece of work. I'm so furious I don't answer either of them but fit the bowl back on the processor along with the shredding blade.

"Anjali, what are you making?" Quade asks. "The audience wants to know."

What is he talking about? There's no audience. Just the parents and the judges.

"I'm going to make a special slaw with jicama and watercress," I say, pulling out the jicama from the fridge. I peel it and slice it into chunks that I shove into the funnel of the processor.

"Fifteen minutes to service!" Brenda calls out from where she's standing behind the lights and cameramen.

I quickly grate a carrot. I chop an onion as fast as I can. I remember back to when I learned how to chop from Deema, her soft arms wrapped around me, guiding my hands. This memory soothes me under these hot lights, with the time clock ticking. I mix everything together with my hands and top it with the sweetened vinegar dressing I've already prepared.

Next come the rotis. I look wildly around for the flat iron griddle called a *tawa* I brought in. *Where is it?* I finally see it at the edge of the counter out of the camera's sight. Someone has rested a half-empty can of soda on my *tawa*. I move the can and grab the *tawa*. I run back to where the camera is and plunk the *tawa* down on the stove, turning the heat on medium.

By now the too-big T-shirt is chafing my underarms and starting to itch. I can't fuss with it. The most important thing right now is to get the food done before my time's up.

While the *tawa* is heating up, I put a frying pan on

the burner beside it and add some oil. I pull out the shrimp mixture from the refrigerator and form it into fat cigars. I've never worked this fast, even on the most packed days at Island Spice.

Out of the corner of my eye I see He Kyong sitting at the big stool at her counter, talking to Quade and the camera. She's pointing to her finished dish and explaining something. Next to her Jimmy is spooning his sauce over the pork chops on three plates. I am nowhere near done. My heart is slamming. I still have to finish making the rotis!

"Two minutes!" Brenda calls.

Pulling the first roti off the *tawa*, I quickly oil up the *tawa* again and throw the second roti on it.

I race as fast as I can — adding shrimp to each roti, slicing tomatoes, sprinkling slaw, rolling up the whole thing like a cone. I reach into a bag of plantain chips and decorate the plate by plunking a mound next to each roti sandwich.

"Time!" Brenda yells.

Shrimp Burger Pitas

1 pound large shrimp, peeled and deveined
2 teaspoons green seasoning (see recipe on
page 102)
1/4 cup heavy cream
1 shallot, minced
1/2 teaspoon salt
freshly ground pepper to taste
1/4 cup canola oil
1 cup cornmeal, or more as needed
4 large pita breads or small rotis
tomato slices for garnish

1. Place the shrimp, green seasoning, and heavy cream in the bowl of a food
processor and pulse to achieve a thick
paste, about 1 minute.
2. Remove the shrimp mixture from the
bowl and add the shallot, salt, and pepper,
and mix well. Chill the mixture for 15
minutes.

3. Heat a large frying pan over medium-high heat and add the canola oil. Remove the shrimp mixture and mold it into patties if using pita, or "cigars," 5 inches long and 2 inches wide, if using rotis.

4. Dredge the shrimp patties in cornmeal and then place them in the frying pan, turning the heat down to medium-low. Cook until lightly browned on all sides, about 3 to 4 minutes. Remove from oil with a slotted spoon and place on a plate lined with paper towels to drain.

5. Place each patty into a pita and garnish with tomato slices, and jicama watercress slaw (see recipe on page 103). If using rotis, place each shrimp "cigar" on a roti, garnish with tomato slices and slaw, and roll up. Serve with cassava or plantain chips on the side.

Makes 4 servings

 # Green Seasoning

3 tablespoons chopped chives

1 tablespoon chopped *shado beni* (Mexican *culantro*) or cilantro

2 tablespoons chopped fresh thyme

1 tablespoon chopped fresh oregano

1 tablespoon chopped fresh parsley

4 cloves garlic, minced

Process all the ingredients in a food processor until the mixture forms a thick paste. Store in a tightly sealed glass jar in the refrigerator for up to a week.

Makes 1 cup

Jicama Watercress Slaw

1/2 cup peeled and shredded jicama

1 carrot, peeled and grated

1/2 bunch watercress, stemmed and chopped roughly

1/4 red chili pepper, minced

1/2 cup rice wine vinegar

2 teaspoons sugar

1. In a medium-size bowl, toss the jicama, carrot, and watercress together so they are well and evenly combined. Set aside.

2. In a smaller bowl, whisk together the chili pepper, rice wine vinegar, and sugar.

3. Pour the dressing over the jicama mixture and toss well. Refrigerate for 20 minutes. Serve on sandwiches or toss with coleslaw. Works well as a condiment on shrimp burger pitas.

Serves 4

CHAPTER EIGHT

Challenge

I step back and wipe my hands on my side towel. I really want to wipe my sweaty face but that'll smear the makeup. I blow a loose hair from my eyes, take a deep breath, and wait for directions.

Three production assistants walk up with large trays on which they put each contestant's dish to bring to the judges.

The judges sample everything at the same time.

After they've finished sampling, they nod to Brenda, who says, "Contestants, please step in front of the judges."

My insides are still pumping.

"I'll start with He Kyong's dish," says Daisy Martinez. "The mushroom salad is lovely, refreshing, light," she begins. "I love the flavor combination but I might have liked to see it paired with something crisp to counteract its soft texture rather than the soft noodles."

He Kyong has not stopped smiling.

"I thought it was just delicious!" Sam says. "Good job!"

"I'm not a big mushroom fan," says Connor. "But I can see how hard you worked on it, so I'm giving it a thumbs-up!"

Daisy Martinez looks over the top of her reading glasses at Connor like she's about to say something, but keeps it rolling.

"Now, Anjali's sandwich," she says. "I thought this was very unusual — in a good way. I enjoyed the flavors and the bread. It's not quite like a pita."

"It's roti," I say too softly. I clear my throat and try again. "It's roti; it's a Trinidadian bread. They make it in Guyana, too. It came from India originally."

"Well, it's awesome. I love it," says Daisy. "And the jicama slaw is really a stroke of genius. You pulled off a complex dish in a short time. I think you are going to be a remarkable young chef. Good job, *mija*!" She smiles real big, and I feel all of me smiling, too.

"Yeah, the roti is delicious!" Sam says.

"It *was* good," says Connor. "Like a souvlaki sandwich or a falafel or something."

Daisy Martinez turns to Jimmy.

"So, young man, your pork chops," she says.

"My grandmother's," Jimmy corrects with a small laugh.

"Yes, your grandmother's," Daisy says. "They needed a little something. . . ."

Jimmy looks angry.

"Have you considered maybe a bit of hot pepper? Or perhaps some paprika? It needs a little oomph," she says.

"No, that's how my grandmother makes it." Jimmy folds his arms. "Everyone else likes it just as it is."

"I'm sure they do — what's better than a meal from a Brooklyn Italian grandma?" says Daisy. "I'm just giving you a suggestion to elevate your chops from like to love."

"I thought they tasted great!" Sam says.

I bite my lip because I really want to laugh. Sam thinks everything tastes great.

Daisy ignores Sam and goes on. "Jimmy, part of being a chef is being willing to adapt your dish to your guests' tastes."

"I love pork chops," cuts in Connor. "So they were totally cool by me."

"Thanks, man!" Jimmy says, holding up his fist and punching the air toward Connor.

"Okay, contestants," calls out Brenda. Apparently the camera is now off. "We're going to take fifteen. Before your break, though, let's do the market basket reveal."

We go back to our areas and stand expectantly while Quade comes back onstage. The camera comes back on, but only for a moment.

"And now it's time for the market basket challenge!" Quade says to the camera. "Each contestant will have to come up with an original dish using the ingredients here." He pulls the white cloth off the tray to reveal salmon, rice, and lemons. "Let's see what these cooking kids come up with after the break!"

The cameras go dark again.

"Fifteen minutes," Brenda calls.

I untie my apron and walk over to Nyla. She hugs me.

"You're doing great, Anjali!" she says. "How do you feel?"

"The market basket is making me nervous."

Nyla squares my shoulders with both her hands. She helps me tuck in my shirt. "Anjali," she says, "remember, you have a gift for cooking."

I try to nod, but all I can do is blow more loose hair from my eyes.

"A gift," Nyla repeats.

When I get back to the kitchen, I open the refrigerator on the set and look at the ingredients I have left. There are lemons and some callaloo leaves. I also think of a way to use my own soy ginger glaze.

At that moment, I get the very thing Nyla's been saying all along — a gift. I know exactly what I'll do for the market basket challenge! I like my idea so much that I can't wait for the second half of the contest to begin. The ingredients play like a song in my mind: *salmon, rice, callaloo, lemons*. When the camera rolls, I'm ready.

I get a small pot of rice going and then fill a pan with water, dice some lemon with the peel, add a bit of sugar, and let the whole thing simmer. While it's boiling down, I get the salmon under the broiler, basting it every five minutes with my soy ginger glaze so the flavor is sure to be intense. I set a big pot of salted water on the stove to blanch the callaloo leaves, but the leaves are nowhere. I race over to the refrigerator — maybe I only thought I took them out. But they aren't there, either.

I look around frantically. All of a sudden that pest Quade is beside me.

"You look like you're on a mission, Anjali!" he booms in my ear. "What're you hunting for?" He's talking to the camera. I ignore him. The cameraman follows me as I pass Jimmy, who is so into chopping up some garlic that his tongue is sticking out of the side of his mouth like some goofy cartoon character.

I go over to He Kyong's area. She has her back to us and is trying to quickly chop something.

"Aaargh!" She drops the knife and sucks her finger.

I dash around to the front of her board. There are *my* callaloo leaves, chopped to pieces!

"What do you think you're doing?" I yell, snatching up what's left of my callaloo. She shrugs and gives another smile and winks at the camera.

"It's all about sharing, right, Anjali?" she says. "I thought I'd try something new."

I look over at Quade, who is watching the whole thing, then at the judges, who are straining to get a better look at what's going on.

"Stealing is not new," I hiss.

I stomp back to my station and pull my water and lemon off the stove so it won't burn. I quickly trim the stems of the remaining callaloo leaves and throw the leaves into the pot. I'm making something that's never been done before — salmon callaloo sushi rolls.

I make the rolls faster than I've made anything ever. There's a minute to spare when time is called. I look over and see that He Kyong has done some kind of fried rice using chopped salmon and callaloo. She's garnished the rice with lemon slices. And as far as I can tell, Jimmy just baked the salmon and squeezed lemon and herbs over it, with the rice on the side and a dollop of butter. *Boring.*

"Let's start with the salmon rolls," says Daisy Martinez. "I thought this was a good effort. Very creative. The final result was a little too sweet — I'd cut back on the sugar in the marinade. But otherwise good — especially given your, ah, difficulties." She looks over her glasses at He Kyong.

"Very tasty!" says Sam Vitelli. "I'd only say that it seemed too similar to your other dish — both of them being roll-like thingies. But otherwise, delicious."

"Yeah, I'm not a fan of salmon," says Connor Sebastian. "So this wasn't for me."

Even with Connor's stupid non-comments, I'm feeling confident now. The callaloo sushi rolls are a cool idea. I know this.

Daisy gives her opinion on He Kyong's fried rice.

"The ginger is a wonderful addition, and I never would have thought of doing a fried rice with salmon. Great job!"

"Totally yummy!" says Sam, smiling at He Kyong.

"I agree," says Connor. "I could barely taste the salmon!"

Could this guy *get* any stupider?

"Now for Jimmy's salmon and rice," says Daisy. "This was a solid dish. Simple but still good. The flavor of this beautiful fresh salmon wasn't altered, and that's a good thing. I would have liked to see you try and stretch a bit with the rice. But good job!"

Jimmy looks happy.

"I loved the herbs! Tasted wonderful!" says Sam.

"Dude, it was practically like a steak," says Connor. "And who doesn't like steak?" He laughs at his own joke, and Jimmy laughs, too.

Quade suddenly appears at the end of the judges' table and faces his own camera. "Who will win this round of *Super Chef Kids*? Tune in next week when the finalists square off in the final elimination round when the star of our next season is crowned!"

He continues to smile widely at the camera until Brenda calls out, "Wrap!"

I thank Nyla, who holds me for a long minute. "Anjali, you're already a star," she says, "no matter what happens."

I'm exhausted when I head out into the snowy street. I realize I've left my Island Spice T-shirt at the studio. I'll keep my coat on over this sloppy yellow shirt, then hide the thing later. Hopefully, no one will notice.

Glancing at my watch, I see it's nearly noon. Linc will be done with the Stuyvesant test by now. I open my umbrella and walk the three avenues to Union Square so I can grab a subway downtown to Stuyvesant High School in Battery Park.

Trini-Style Salmon Sushi Rolls

1/4 cup soy sauce

2 tablespoons sugar or honey

1 tablespoon mirin (sweet rice wine)

1/4 teaspoon five-spice powder

1 pound boneless, skinless salmon

1 teaspoon salt

4 large callaloo leaves, stem ends trimmed

1 small lemon, washed well

1/3 cup water

1 tablespoon toasted sesame seed oil

1/2 cup cooked white rice, preferably sushi rice, prepared according to the package directions

soy sauce and wasabi mustard for condiment (optional)

1. Preheat the oven to 350 degrees Fahrenheit.

2. Whisk the soy sauce, 2 teaspoons of the sugar or honey, mirin, and five-spice powder together.

3. Place the salmon on a cookie sheet or in an oven-safe dish and brush it all over with the soy sauce mixture.

4. Place the salmon in the oven right underneath the top heating element. Cook for 15 to 20 minutes, basting with the soy sauce mixture every five minutes. Remove from the oven when cooked through, and set aside to cool.

5. While the salmon is cooking, fill a large bowl with 2 cups of ice and 3 cups of water. Bring a large pot of water to boil and add the salt. Add the callaloo leaves and cook for 30 seconds. Remove carefully from the hot water and put the leaves in the ice water. When they are cool, about 30 seconds, remove and lay them carefully on folded paper towels.

6. Make the lemon confit: Cut the lemon into 1/4-inch slices. Carefully remove the

seeds and then chop the slices into small chunks. Place the lemon chunks in a small saucepan with the remaining sugar or honey and 1/3 cup of water. Bring the mixture to a boil and then reduce temperature to bring to a low simmer. Simmer for 15 minutes or until almost all the water has evaporated. Set aside to cool.

7. Make the rolls: Brush the callaloo leaves evenly with sesame seed oil and divide the rice equally among the leaves. Carefully smooth the rice evenly over each leaf, taking care not to tear the leaf.

8. Slice the cooled salmon lengthwise into 4 equal pieces. Place the salmon on top of the rice, toward the edge of the leaf. Repeat with all four leaves. Spoon the lemon confit equally onto each piece of salmon, spooning the mixture down the length of the piece of salmon.

9. Roll the leaf carefully away from you as if you are making a cigar. Try to make the roll fairly tight. Repeat with all four rolls.

10. Place the rolls seam side down on a cutting board and slice them into 1-inch-wide pieces. Serve with a side of soy sauce and wasabi mustard, if desired.

Serves 4 to 6

CHAPTER NINE

Furious

On the Sunday evening right after test day my family sits around our dinner table. It's rare for us all to be eating together at the same time. Mom has finished studying, and our restaurant is closed because Dad and Anand have repainted the walls, which are still wet.

"Ma, you sure have some sweet hand," Dad says to Deema between bites of the duck curry Deema's made for dinner.

We're all talking at the same time, but about different things. Deema's telling Dad about her secret for duck curry and rice — the foods that cover our Sunday dinner table. Mom's talking about her next nursing exam. Anand won't shut up about a new video game that's taken him to level seven.

Dishes clink. I'm quiet, thinking while everyone else eats, talks, talks, talks, and fills the room with the spice of our conversation. Mom's the first to notice that I'm all about downing Deema's duck curry and not saying anything.

"Anjali, child, who's taken your tongue?" she asks. I shrug. Then she zings me with a question I don't want to answer. "Have any of the other kids at school gotten their Stuyvesant results?" My mouth is full of rice. I don't speak. "Some of the families in the Sovalds' building have already got their results," Mom says.

It's hard to swallow, but I manage.

"I don't think anyone at my school has heard from Stuyvesant," I mumble.

Anand says, "My friend's brother Jason got his results."

My dad stops eating. "Maybe we should call the Board of Ed tomorrow, just to see where things are in the process."

My eyes are stuck to my plate. I take a deep breath.

"Dad," I say softly, then look from my father to Deema, "I have something to say." I put down my fork. "You don't have to call the Board of Ed. I didn't get in to Stuyvesant."

"Why didn't you tell us? Where's the letter?" Dad wants to know.

"There wasn't a letter."

"How yuh mean there wasn't a letter?" Dad's voice is rising.

There's disappointment on Dad's face. Mom's, too. Deema folds her arms. She's looking at me curiously.

"I never took the test," I whisper.

"What?" Mom looks like I've told her there's a rat in the room.

Anand leans across the table. "Whoa."

"I never took it. I went to the tryout for the Food Network show instead," I admit.

"How yuh mean?" my dad says. There's anger in his voice.

"The tryout at the Food Network for the *Super Chef Kids* show." I'm talking fast and furious. "I know you said no, but this is the chance of a lifetime to get my own TV show. I can take the Stuyvesant test next year." Then I tell them about bringing Chef Nyla with me to the audition as my "guardian."

"You did what?" Now Dad's looking like I've committed a crime. Mom's shaking her head. She can't believe what she's hearing. Deema looks disappointed, hurt.

Anand covers his mouth with his hand. He's mumbling something I can't hear.

"Anand, eat your food!" Mom says sharply. "Anjali, what on earth were you thinking?" she asks.

Dad is barely holding on to his fury. "That test at Stuyvesant was your future."

"If I can get my own TV show, it won't matter where I go to school," I say pleadingly. "Imagine how much money I'll make. I'll be a famous chef!"

Dad starts tapping his fork on the table while I speak.

"I done told yuh I had enough of this chef business, and now this." His voice is so quiet, scarier than when he's yelling. "Your hobby has turned yuh into a cheat and a liar."

"But —"

He puts up his hand. "No, stop talking now. I don't want to hear anything more about this. You will not watch any more cooking shows. Yuh only gonna prepare food in our shop. No more special cooking or cooking classes. This is over."

"But —" I look at Deema. "Deema, please, I —"

Deema shakes her head. Her eyes are moist.

"Listen to your father, child," she says quietly.

This is all too much. Even Deema is ganging up on me.

"You'll change your mind when I win!" I burst out. "Let's see what you say when *that* letter comes!"

"Get up from the table now, Anjali," my father says, pushing his plate away and standing up.

I stare furiously at Dad, then at my mother and Deema. I give Anand an evil look, too.

I stand up quickly, knowing my chair will fall backward. "You don't care about what I want! If you love Stuyvesant so much, why don't *you* go there!"

I run to my room and slam the door, kicking it once, hard, from the inside.

Spicy Fried Channa (Chickpeas)

1/4 teaspoon freshly ground black pepper

1/4 teaspoon cayenne pepper

3/4 teaspoon coarse salt

1/2 teaspoon onion powder

1/2 teaspoon garlic powder

1 cup canola oil

1 fifteen-ounce can chickpeas, drained and dried in a salad spinner or with paper towels

1. In a small bowl, whisk together the black pepper, cayenne pepper, salt, and onion and garlic powders. Set aside.

2. Heat the oil in a deep frying pan on medium heat until a deep-frying thermometer reaches 375 degrees Fahrenheit, or until a pinch of flour dropped into the pan sizzles.

3. Carefully add the chickpeas by gently spooning them into the frying pan using a long-handled metal spoon. Place a splatter screen over the frying pan. The chickpeas will splatter and pop quite a bit while frying.

4. Allow the chickpeas to fry for 3 to 4 minutes or until their outsides begin to look golden brown. Remove the chickpeas from the pan using a slotted spoon and place them on a large tray lined with paper towels.

5. When all the chickpeas are fried, place them in a deep bowl and add the spice mixture, stirring well so that all of the chickpeas are coated. Allow to cool. Serve as a snack.

Makes 4 servings

CHAPTER TEN

Hope

After school, I walk slowly down Liberty Avenue toward Island Spice. I hate working at our shop now, with my father speaking to me only to give orders.

The worst part is not being able to go to the culinary school to work with Nyla. I called to tell her how my family reacted to my audition, and I told her the truth about missing the test at Stuyvesant. She was so disappointed in me. Even so, I miss her.

I walk into Island Spice and pass my father on my way to the back room, where I dump my stuff. Dad's busy talking to customers.

I go to the worktable, where Deema is shredding salted codfish for the next morning's breakfast.

"Hi, Deema."

"Bayti," she says. "Something came for you in the mail. It looks important."

Deema dries her hands on the side towel looped through her apron strings and goes into the back room. She comes out holding an envelope.

The envelope says Scripps on it. That means Food Network. My stomach lurches.

"It's from the Food Network, Deema." My mouth is dry.

Deema puts down the knife she's holding.

"Well, open it."

I force the envelope open with my finger, tearing the flap unevenly. I tug at the letter inside.

Dear Ms. Krishnan:

It's my pleasure to inform you that you are the New York finalist for Super Chef Kids.

I stop reading and scream.

"What, what is it?" Deema is alarmed. Dad comes running.

"I made it! I made it!" I'm jumping up and down and waving the letter. "I'm a finalist!"

"For that show?" my father asks.

"Yes!" I say, flapping the envelope. "I told you! See? It *was* worth it!"

Dad crosses his arms. "What else it say?"

I finish reading the letter. "It says the finals are

three weeks from Saturday and that I'm the kid chef chosen from the New York area."

I read further, silently to myself. Like the other letter, it says I have to bring a parent or guardian. I look nervously at my father. I read this part out loud to him.

Dad storms out of the room.

"Deema, you'll go with me, right?" I ask.

She picks up her knife. "Let's see what happens, darlin'."

I worry for the rest of the evening while I clean tables, help Deema trim vegetables, and dish out food for customers.

When things get quiet, Deema and I sit down to eat our own dinner. I'm not hungry.

I get up to bring our plates inside and pass the door to our shop's office, where my father's on the phone, behind a closed door. It sounds like he's talking to my mother.

"Can you believe it?" he's saying. "I know that the girl can cook, for true." He pauses.

I stand there frozen for a few seconds before I realize I better move or I'll get caught listening.

Later, at home, I'm in bed, trying to sleep. It's way past midnight. Dad has just come from the shop. Mom's studying. The house is quiet, so I can hear Mom and Dad talking.

"I've been thinking," Dad says to Mom.

"Me, too," says Mom.

"About Anjali and this cooking show?" Dad asks.

"It's been on my mind all day," says Mom.

I hear rustling. The floorboards creak. "Nobody invite me to this party," says Deema. "So I invite myself."

Mom says, "We're talking about Anjali."

"*Bayti,*" says Deema. "That child has been given to us by the heavens as special gift. She know her way 'round the kitchen — and she full of spice, too."

"She gets that from her father," Mom says.

"She get that from all of us," Deema says. "We from the island where everything spicy."

Dad says, "Anjali has betrayed us with her dishonesty."

"She shouldn't have lied," says Deema. "But we betray Anjali by not letting her have her joy, and by denying her the gift heaven has given her to share with others. That is a betrayal worse than lying."

There's silence.

Deema keeps talking. "You want to be a nurse," she says to Mom. "You study. You work hard. When you become a nurse, you'll help people feel good. The same for Anjali. The way she cook — with ideas flowing from her like the sweet water from a coconut — also helps people feel good."

Dad tries to get a word in. "But she —"

Deema stops him. "But she works so hard for you at the shop — serving, wiping tables, smiling at customers. Now it's our turn to work for her. Our girl. Our *bayti*."

"How yuh mean, work?" Dad asks.

"Work past your stubbornness," Deema says.

More quiet.

Then Dad speaks. "One thing I know," he says. "We not quitters in this family. Anjali's started something, and now she must finish it."

"For true," says Deema.

My mom brushes something only she can see from my shirt and fusses with the tie on my apron. I'm back at the Food Network studios. This time Mom and Deema have come with me, while Dad works at the shop. Mom, Deema, and I stand with the other two finalists in the greenroom, waiting to go out to the set.

This time my opponents are a guy who looks to be sixteen and a girl about seventeen. I'm the youngest contestant.

The guy, Randolph, has a Mohawk. His lip is pierced with three rings. He's wearing black nail polish, a black T-shirt, black jeans, black sneakers, and a black apron. The girl, who is called Brooklyn but is actually from California, is blond and calls herself a surfer chick.

Deema seems to be enjoying herself, talking a lot to Randolph, asking about his piercings.

Mom keeps adjusting my clothes and hair.

I'm nervous about this contest. It's a market basket, right from the beginning. I'm not going to be able to cook something I've prepared before, and I'm worried all over again that the ingredients will be something I never cook, like beef or pork.

Anyway, I'm not too sure what I would do if that happens. When I tell this to Deema she suggests that I prepare beef or pork the same way I'd make a dish with chicken. Good idea, but I still don't feel confident.

Brenda comes hustling in, outfitted with her microphone and black box.

"Okay, contestants, this is it," she says. "Follow me."

When we get to the studio, she shows the parents where to sit. The judges wave at us as we file past them. When we get to the kitchen area, we're each assigned a station, same as before.

Quade is ready with his mic in place, and before I know it, they're counting down to filming.

I look over at the judges. Daisy Martinez is there with Sam Vitelli and Connor Sebastian. They're sitting forward, looking very eager. My head is starting to hurt.

Quade is talking now, so I turn my focus to him.

"Our finalists will be cooking an original creation from a list of secret ingredients we are about to reveal." He pauses, then dramatically pulls a white cloth off a tray of ingredients. There's some reddish meat, red and green peppers, bacon, creole rice, and chilies. "The main ingredient our contestants will have to work with tonight is rabbit tenderloins! Don't go away, folks. We'll be right back as the kitchen heats up here on *Super Chef Kids*!"

I feel dizzy, like I'm going to throw up. I never in my life thought of rabbit as anything but a cute fuzzy pet. *Rabbit?* I turn around so I'm not facing the judges and blow air out of my mouth. *What am I going to do with rabbit?*

Get ahold of yourself, Anjali, I'm thinking. But the rabbit thing has thrown me for too much of a loop.

I focus on the creole rice, which we make with chicken in my house. At least I know it can be adapted.

"And we're back for the final showdown between our young contestants," Quade is saying. "The three young people — Anjali, Randolph, and Brooklyn — beat out some amazing young cooks from around the country to get here."

While Quade talks, I start to gather the ingredients I need from the refrigerator and the staples pantry.

Peanut butter, onions, garlic, tomato. I start dicing the peppers. I add chopped onions for extra flavor.

Randolph is stroking his chin and nodding before he dashes off and starts rummaging through his own pantry. Brooklyn is carefully sharpening a filleting knife.

Quade is by my side, talking. "Anjali impressed the judges last time. Can she do it again?"

Before I can say anything, he's dashed off. *Good*, I think, *it's easier to cook without him bugging me.*

I heat a heavy pot and add the chopped onions and pepper. I glance up at my mother and Deema, who look worried. I close my eyes and try to focus by concentrating on the smell the onions give off while they cook — sweet, pungent, soothing, reminding me of home.

When the onions are soft, I add the bacon. I'm winging it now, based on what I've learned watching TV shows. I've never cooked bacon before. Quade is talking to Brooklyn, who is pounding what looks like the rabbit meat. At his station, Randolph has gotten out a food processor and is grinding the meat into a paste while he fries up the bacon on the stove.

I look down at my pot. There's too much oil. The bacon released a lot of fat. I look around in a panic and grab a pot spoon. I'll have to skim off some of the fat or the dish will be too greasy. I grab the handle of the iron pot to tilt it forward but drop it fast. I've forgotten to use my side towel to grip the hot handle. The pot lands on the stove with a loud clatter. I step away, stamping my foot.

Quade is at my station. "Looks like our New York contender is having a bit of trouble today," he says into the camera. "The pressure is on!"

I reach into the freezer and grab some ice for my hand. But only for a few seconds. I have to keep cooking.

I'm not sure how, but I manage to grit through the pain and grab the pot handle — this time with my towel — so I can skim off the fat. I wash my hands, cut the rabbit tenderloins into one-inch cubes as fast as I can, and throw those into the pot. The rabbit smell makes me sick. But I keep going, stirring until the meat is brown on all sides.

I add water, tomato, and peanut butter and let the whole thing simmer. The problem is I don't know how long rabbit needs to cook. I'll have to guess because I'm not going to taste it because of the bacon. In the meantime, I wash the rice and drain it, adding it to the pot with two of the red chilies, which I drop in whole.

I stir the whole thing, lower the heat to a simmer, and glance at the clock. The dish isn't complicated, so I'll have to dress it up somehow.

Randolph is mixing something in a bowl with his hands, talking and gesturing to the camera. Little pieces of meat fly off his fingers every time he moves his hands. Brooklyn is bending over her fillet, which is seasoned. She's slowly smearing it with something pink.

I chop parsley as a garnish for my dish, but what else can I serve with it? I rummage through the staples pantry and find some red cabbage, which I use to make a quick slaw.

I check the creole rice. So far, so good. I leave the cover off so the water can evaporate.

"Five minutes!" Quade calls out, then moves closer to the camera to add more commentary. I look up at my mom and Deema, who are sitting forward anxiously and looking at me with so much love.

I fluff the rice with a fork, then poke through one of the pieces of rabbit. It seems cooked, but it's a little tougher than I expected. I put the rice, rabbit, and slaw on a plate, then garnish the whole thing with chopped parsley.

There's a vase of orchids sitting on the counter between me and Randolph. I pluck three small flowers and put them on the side of my plated food.

I smile to myself. My dish looks pretty. Quade calls out, "Time!"

I take a breath and sip some water. *Whew!*

"Contestants, please step forward," Quade says. We all walk up to the judges' table.

Brooklyn goes first. She's made some kind of little roll with the rabbit and wrapped it in bacon.

"Tell us about your dish," Chef Daisy says.

Brooklyn gives her a big smile. "Well, Chef, I pounded out the rabbit tenderloin into a fillet and stuffed it with a mousseline I made with roasted red pepper and a little cream. Then I wrapped the whole thing in bacon and broiled it."

Brooklyn's dish looks pretty professional.

The judges each taste some of their plates. There's a look of surprise on Sam Vitelli's face.

"This really is good!" she exclaims. It's funny to see her react genuinely to something, though it makes me worry about my dish.

"Very beautiful presentation and skillfully done," says Chef Daisy. "Thumbs-up!"

Connor Sebastian still has his mouth full. "This is totally awesome," he says between chews.

Next, it's my turn.

Chef Daisy tastes first. She chews, then chews more. She's thinking. Sam Vitelli hesitantly tries hers. She makes a face like *ewww*. Connor Sebastian takes a quick nibble, then puts his fork down.

Daisy folds her hands on the table.

"The flavors in this dish are amazing, Anjali," she says. "But the rabbit is tough."

This feels like a kick in the stomach. Daisy had liked me so much before.

"Yeah, it didn't really gel with me," says Sam Vitelli. "Nice presentation, though."

"Little too spicy for me," says Connor Sebastian.

I nod miserably and step back. Randolph comes forward. He's made little dumplings with a meat filling he's created. There's a dipping sauce of rice wine vinegar and bacon bits.

"Very tasty," Chef Daisy says, smiling at him. "You pulled this together in such a short time, too. Well done!"

Sam Vitelli agrees. "Tastes great!"

Connor says the dish is "cool."

"Okay, folks, that's a wrap!" Brenda calls out.

When I go to Mom and Deema, they're both eager to hug me.

Creole Rice

1/4 pound bacon, diced

1 small onion, chopped

1 green bell pepper, stemmed, seeded, and cut into strips

1 small red bell pepper, stemmed, seeded, and cut into strips

1 Roma tomato, chopped

1/2 pound stew beef, cut into 1-inch cubes

1 tablespoon peanut butter

2 1/2 cups beef or chicken stock

1/4 Scotch bonnet pepper, minced, or more to taste

1 cup parboiled rice (such as Uncle Ben's)

fresh chopped parsley for garnish

1. Heat a skillet and place the bacon in it. Fry for 5 minutes, then add the onion and the green and red bell peppers and chopped tomato. Sauté for 1 to 2 minutes, or until

the onion is soft. Add the beef cubes and toss well to coat. Lightly brown the beef on all sides. Mix well and fry for 5 minutes, stirring often.

2. Stir in the peanut butter and mix thoroughly. Add the stock and stir well. Reduce the heat to a simmer and cook for 15 minutes.

3. Mix in the Scotch bonnet pepper and rice. Reduce the heat to medium-low, cover, and simmer until the rice is thoroughly cooked and all the liquid is absorbed. The rice should not be sticky. Serve on a platter, garnished with the parsley.

Makes 4 servings

CHAPTER ELEVEN
Disappointment

I scramble through my backpack to answer the phone, which is buried somewhere beneath all my books. As I see the bus heading down the street, I kneel on the ground to search more frantically.

The phone is on the sixth ring by the time I get to it. It's a 212 number. I press the phone to my ear. "Hello?" I say breathlessly.

"Yes, hello, I'd like to speak with Anjali Krishnan," a man's voice says on the other end.

"This is Anjali."

"Curtis Whitmore from the Food Network." The voice comes through clearly but starts to break up.

The bus begins to roll toward me with its rumbling engine. My mouth goes dry with excitement. I walk quickly around the corner to a quieter part of the street.

"Hi," I say, pacing nervously.

"Ms. Krishnan, I'm calling about your audition for the *Super Chef Kids* show."

I have an uncontrollable urge to giggle. "Yes?" I say.

"Ms. Krishnan, everyone loved you. You did a great job." I bounce on my feet to relieve some of my nervous excitement. What I really want to do is run and yell and laugh at the same time.

"But we've decided that one of the other candidates fits what we're looking for a little better," he says.

I stop moving and stand very still. I'm dizzy, disoriented, like when I've been swimming too long and finally step out of the pool. The world seems shaky. I can't trust my own feet to take a sure step.

"*What?*" I ask stupidly.

"I'm sorry, Ms. Krishnan. We're going with one of the other candidates."

I can't believe what I'm hearing. *They are actually calling to say no? Why didn't they just send a letter?* "Oh?" is all I can manage.

He's still talking, saying how much they enjoyed meeting me, but disappointment and anger have filled me up.

"Who won?" I blurt.

The voice on the other end of the phone is silent for a few beats.

"Well, that's why I'm calling," he says overly cheerfully. "We'd like all the finalists to be there for the reveal."

I don't answer.

"Then the final show will air on Labor Day so you can watch yourself," he says quickly. "You'll be getting a FedEx tomorrow or the next day with details about coming in. I'm calling to give you a heads-up. The reveal will likely be filmed at some point in the next few weeks."

"Uh-huh," I barely mumble. *Is he kidding?*

"Okay, then, talk to you soon!" Curtis Whitmore chirps before disconnecting.

I stand there a few minutes after the call is over, only moving when a mother pushes past me with a double stroller. Two young boys ride by on their bikes, yelling back and forth and laughing.

I walk back to the bus stop. It starts to fill up. I bend over on the bench, rest my head in my hands, and sob.

I go straight to Linc's house. His housekeeper, Marisol, greets me at the door.

"Anjali! *Hola!* Come in, come in!"

I step inside.

"Linc is on the back patio." She closes the door behind me. "Go on through."

"Hey, Linc," I say quietly.

"Anjali?" he says, sitting up abruptly. "What are you doing here?"

I try to get the words out but the only thing I can do is cry. Finally, I say, "Food Network called to tell me they picked someone else."

"Wait, what?" Linc looks surprised. "Who'd they pick?"

"I don't know. They want me to come back to film a reveal when they choose the winner!" I'm really crying hard. I wipe my face with the back of my hand.

"I've screwed up everything!" I wipe my eyes again. "No Stuyvesant, no Food Network show, no more culinary school. Nothing."

Linc leans forward and grabs my shoulder. "Hey, hey, take it easy. It's not so bad."

He hands me a tissue.

"With you being so wrapped up in the TV stuff, I never got to tell you — I didn't get in to Stuyvesant. At least we'll be in school together next year."

"So we're both losers," I say, trying to manage a smile.

Linc laughs.

"I'd been hoping to go to the local high school so I could do a C-CAP program," I say. "I know, I know — crazy," I blurt before Linc can say anything.

"Crazy Anjali," Linc says. Then, "We may be losers, but we still got *pow*."

That makes me laugh for real.

It's twilight when I finally reach home. Mom is standing at the stove, stirring something. I can smell the sweetness of coconut, along with the warm spiciness of mixed essence and the salty, woodsy smell of rice all jumbled together. Rice pudding.

Mom turns as I come into the kitchen. There's a frown creasing her eyebrows. "Where have you —" she begins but stops quickly. My face is puffy from crying.

"Anjali, honey, what's wrong?"

I slump down in a kitchen chair and put my head in my hands.

"I didn't win the Food Network tryout," I say miserably. "They chose someone else. Now you can say you told me so."

My mom turns off the pot of rice pudding and comes to sit by me. She strokes my hair. "Anjali, look at me."

It feels like a million years since we've been alone together. I can't remember the last time I saw Mom cook anything.

"I'm not going to say I told you so. You've shown me what it means to have passion, Anjali. Thank you for teaching me such a valuable lesson."

"What about Dad?" I ask. "He's going to get mad all over again."

"Oh, sweetie," Mom says. She puts both her arms around me. "He's not mad anymore. I know it's hard for you to understand, but he didn't want you to get hurt, to be disappointed. He's a proud man."

Deema's voice comes into the kitchen from where she stands at the doorway. "This whole family is stubborn, *bayti*. But we love you. You make us so proud.

"I think we could all use a little sweetness right about now," Deema says. She goes to Mom's pot. "Who's up for a taste?"

Sweet Rice
(Coconut Rice Pudding)

1 cup long-grain rice

1 1/2 cups water

1 1/2 cups coconut milk

1/2 cup sugar

pinch of cinnamon

pinch of nutmeg

1/4 teaspoon vanilla extract

1/4 teaspoon mixed essence

1/2 teaspoon Angostura bitters

2 tablespoons raisins (optional)

1 tablespoon sweetened coconut flakes for garnish (optional)

1. Place the rice in a large bowl and add enough water to cover the rice by 2 or 3 inches. Using your hand, swirl the rice around until the water becomes cloudy, then carefully pour the water off the rice.

Repeat this process 4 or 5 times or until the water runs clear.

2. Bring 1 1/2 cups of water to a boil and add the rice. Simmer for 15 minutes, skimming any foam from the top of the rice, as necessary.

3. Drain the rice and return it to the saucepan. Add the coconut milk, sugar, cinnamon, and nutmeg. Simmer for 10 minutes, then add the vanilla, mixed essence, bitters, and raisins if using. Simmer for 10 minutes more. The rice should be soft, and the pudding should be thick but not sticky, with some liquid.

4. Garnish with the coconut flakes and serve.

Makes 4 servings

PART

THREE

REDEMPTION

Recipe for Redemption

2 parts understanding, sliced
1 part forgiveness
1/2 cup temperance
1 second chance
sprinkles of hope as garnish

1. Preheat oven to 350 degrees Fahrenheit.
2. Grease a large casserole dish and layer the understanding along the bottom. Dot with large spoonfuls of forgiveness and repeat until both are entirely used.
3. Pour the temperance over the casserole and season with the second chance.
4. Bake covered for as long as it takes to be cooked through and release a satisfying aroma. Serve sprinkled with hope, as desired.

CHAPTER TWELVE

Sweet

Once again I find myself in the greenroom at the Food Network studios. They've put me in another stupid yellow T-shirt. I really don't want to be here filming the reveal of who won the contest.

Only Deema's come with me this time. Mom had to work. It's just the two of us in our own greenroom. The other contestants have private rooms, too. I guess they don't want us talking to each other before the show, so we can act surprised. I don't see how the other loser can act surprised, just like I don't know how I can. This will be a real test in faking it. All I want is for today to be over.

They just finished doing my makeup. In the mirror I look all caked up with foundation and lipstick.

A production assistant pokes his head in the room. "Okay, we're ready for you." Deema and I follow him.

When we get to the studio, there's a big sign — *Super Chef Kids!*

Brooklyn and Randolph are already there, each

standing on a little platform of their own. There's a platform left for me.

I take my place and pull in a deep breath. Brooklyn gives me a finger wave, and I do my best to smile at her. Randolph gives me a thumbs-up.

Brenda walks onto the stage. "Okay, kids. We'll begin in five. We are going to show some footage of you cooking from your two tryouts, then the judges will announce the winner."

We all nod.

Someone on the set calls out, "Ready in five, four, three, two, one!" He points at Quade, who is in his place, smiling.

"It's the part of the show we've been waiting for, folks, when we learn who is the first-ever *Super Chef Kids* winner! We have our judges . . ."

He introduces the judges, then the three of us, saying our names and where we're from. Next, they break for a commercial, even though this is not really live television.

"I'm Quade Jerome, coming to you from the Food Network studios in New York City," he says when we come back on the air. "We're here to reveal the winner of *Super Chef Kids*! Let's see what these kids can do." He turns toward a massive screen behind us. We have to turn to look, too.

They start by showing Brooklyn at her first tryout, racing around, dropping some stuff, cooking. In between scenes of her cooking, they show scenes from her interview, where she says things like, "Cooking is what calms me, it's my Zen." The camera then cuts to the judges tasting her food and making comments.

There's a commercial, then it's my turn to be humiliated. It's pretty much the same drill for each of us. I wince when I see my interview because I look and sound so stupid. I say, "When I'm a celebrity chef, Caribbean food will be the hottest food around." Ugh! That sounds so preachy.

After they show Randolph's footage, Quade says, "And we'll be back with the winner after this break."

I'm getting tired from standing. I sit on the step behind the little platform. Brooklyn and Randolph do the same thing. None of us speak to each other. Somehow we know we aren't supposed to, I guess.

There's a countdown. We all get to our feet, back on the platforms. "And now, it's time for the judges' decision," says Quade.

The judges step forward in front of us. First is that bubblehead, Sam Vitelli.

She turns toward Brooklyn. "This kid chef worked really hard, made some elegant dishes, and really held it together," she says. "But there was something missing, a certain creativity and pizzazz. Brooklyn, I'm sorry, you're going home."

Brooklyn nods and smiles weakly, giving a wave to the judges and the cameras. She steps down.

I swallow. So Randolph's the winner. I try to play poker face.

Connor Sebastian steps forward next. He's looking at me.

"This young chef showed serious spirit," he says. "No matter what the odds were, this chef kept going. But the food wasn't always approachable and didn't stretch out of a certain comfort zone."

He gestures in my direction. "Anjali, I'm sorry, you're going home."

I turn to Randolph and smile as brightly as I can, then hold out my hand.

"Congratulations!" I say. Randolph looks at me, totally surprised. Maybe he didn't know.

"Wow, uh, wow! Thanks!" He looks dazed. Then suddenly he shakes his head. "Yes!" He raises his arms up in the air.

Chef Daisy steps forward. "Well, the secret is out! Congratulations, Randolph!" She has to stop because he's whooping and hollering so loud. I step away quickly and walk down the platform toward Deema.

"You were inventive and showed great skill for someone so young," Chef Daisy is saying behind me. "Congratulations on getting your own show. I look forward to sharing a stage with you!"

A woman I assume is Randolph's mom races past me with a little girl. They run onstage and hug Randolph like he's just won a game show. They're all jumping up and down and dancing around the set.

I can't move. I'm supposed to walk off the set now,

but my feet won't let me. All the cameras are on Randolph, so nobody can see my makeup melting under the hot lights. Why can't I get over this stupid contest? It's over. Period. I tried and lost. I look for Deema, but she's disappeared.

Brenda comes to where I am and gently leads me back toward my greenroom. "You've got an entourage," she says.

I'm not even halfway down the hall when I see them all lined up in black Island Spice T-shirts from our roti shop — it's Deema, Linc, Anand, Nyla, Mom, and Dad.

They're holding a huge sign that says *POW!* Anand tosses an Island Spice T-shirt at me. "Put this on so people know you're my sister," he says.

I slip the shirt on over the yellow shirt from the network.

Everyone gathers around me. Like Randolph's family, they're jumping and whooping, and they're chanting, "Anjali's got *POW*!"

"Guys," I say, "I didn't win, remember?" I'm giggling.

Linc says, *"Pow* is not about winning — it's about being you."

We all crowd back into the greenroom, where Nyla has a tray arranged with a pitcher of ginger beer and some sweet *prasad* for all of us to eat.

We crowd into the small room, and somehow we all manage to fit.

"You know, Anjali, we have a saying in Trinidad," Deema says. "'One, one cocoa does full basket.' Do you know what that means?"

I sip some ginger beer and shake my head.

"It means that it may take a long time to fill a big basket with cocoa beans, but eventually, if you keep at it, you'll get there. All this is part of that," she says, gesturing around the greenroom. "This is a great learning step. More steps like this will, one by one, get you where you have to go — wherever that may be."

After Deema finishes talking, Mom presses the play button on the iPod speakers she's brought with her. The sounds of David Rudder fill the tiny room as he sings about the hot, sweet joy of island life. Dad gathers me in his arms. He kisses the top of my head. "Sweet Anjali. You make a father happy."

To: Nyla@icecooking.com

From: Masterchef3000@speedcable.net

Dear Chef Nyla — I know, you like me to call you Nyla, but this note is from a soon-to-be chef (me) to a real chef (you):

I had to write and tell you about my first week of school. Richmond Hill High School is totally amazing. There are a lot more kids than at my old school, and it's pretty big. At first I was nervous, but it seems okay now.

Yesterday I finally started the C-CAP part of my curriculum. The first section is going to be on stocks and sauces. Eventually, we are going to learn to do things like cut up meat and fish. The teacher said it's like being in regular culinary school. Pretty cool.

We have regular teachers, but then there are guest teachers — chefs from the big restaurants in the city, even a few Food Network chefs! Last week, Chef Daisy Martinez came to visit!!

Hope to see you soon.

Hugs,

Anjali

I read the e-mail through one more time before I hit send, then sit back in my chair. The smell of the curried mango that Deema is making for the family seeps into my room from the kitchen. I take a deep breath and stretch.

Ginger Beer

8 ounces fresh ginger, peeled and grated on
the large holes of a box grater
2 tablespoons fresh lime juice
1/4 teaspoon ground mace
1 1/2 cups light brown sugar
12 cups water
1/2 vanilla bean, split lengthwise
6 sprigs mint for garnish

1. Put the ginger, lime juice, mace, and
1 1/2 cups of the light brown sugar
into an 8-quart pot and add 12 cups
of water. Bring to a simmer over
medium heat.
2. Scrape the seeds from the vanilla bean
into the pot and add the pod.
3. Stir until the sugar dissolves. Remove
from heat and set aside to cool.

4. Pour the cooled ginger mixture into a widemouthed gallon jug to steep. Cover the jar tightly and refrigerate for 1 week.

5. Strain the ginger mixture through a fine-mesh sieve into another widemouthed gallon glass or ceramic jar, firmly pressing on the solids with the back of a spoon to extract as much flavor as possible. Discard the solids.

6. Serve in glasses over crushed ice, garnished with mint sprigs. Ginger beer may be stored in a sealable glass jar, refrigerated, for up to 2 weeks.

Makes 8 to 10 eight-ounce servings.

Prasad

2 cups ghee (clarified butter)

1/2 cup golden raisins

2 cups farina

2 cups whole milk

3 twelve-ounce cans evaporated milk

4 cups sugar

1 teaspoon peeled and grated fresh ginger

1 teaspoon ground cardamom

Raisins, grated fresh coconut, coarsely chopped almonds, and a few cooked chickpeas, for garnish

1. Heat all but 2 teaspoons of the ghee in a large, deep frying pan. Add the golden raisins and fry over medium-low heat until they become plump.

2. Add the farina one-quarter cup at a time, stirring constantly, until it becomes light brown.

3. While the farina is toasting, in a separate pan, combine the whole milk, evaporated milk, sugar, ginger, and cardamom. Bring just to a boil, stirring constantly. Remove from the heat and add the milk mixture to the farina mixture, one-quarter cup at a time, until the *prasad* forms semimoist clumps.

4. Remove from the heat.

5. Heat the remaining ghee in a small frying pan, and add the raisins, coconut, almonds, and chickpeas. Fry until the raisins are plump, about 30 to 40 seconds. Stir while frying. Garnish the *prasad* with this mixture.

Makes 4 to 6 servings

BONUS RECIPE – Success

5 cups togetherness
4 pounds hard work
ambition as needed
equal measure of reality
liberal sprinkling of joy
satisfaction for finishing the dish

1. Put the togetherness and hard work into the large bowl of a food processor. Pulse evenly until well combined.

2. Remove the mixture from the bowl and knead lightly. Roll out into a large flat round that covers the entire work surface.

3. Walking around the table, spoon big dollops of ambition on the surface of the round. Spoon out enough reality to match ambition equally.

4. Sprinkle liberally with joy and allow to sit for a few days.

5. Garnish with just enough satisfaction to sweeten, and serve generously.

Author's Note

With the exception of my friend and colleague Chef Daisy Martinez, the characters and places in this tale are fictional. However, readers familiar with New York City, particularly Manhattan and Queens, will recognize the terrain of Richmond Hill, the Indo-Caribbean neighborhood where Anjali lives; Forest Hills, where she goes to school; and Manhattan's Chelsea, where the Food Network is located. Certain locales such as Chelsea Market, Stuyvesant High School, and the Institute of Culinary Education are, in fact, real places. While the entrance exam to Stuyvesant High School, or Specialized High School Admissions Test as it is more properly called, is a real event, I have taken liberties with the time the test is given for the purposes of the story. The other characters and events in this story are entirely fictional and bear no resemblance to real people, though I hope readers will find some piece of themselves in this story. Some recipes appearing here were originally published in *Sweet Hands: Island Cooking from Trinidad & Tobago* (Hippocrene Books, © Ramin Ganeshram 2006; second edition 2010).

Acknowledgments

The greatest measure of my thanks goes to my editor, Andrea Pinkney, who saw the potential of this story when it was only a germ of an idea and whose boundless excitement for this work has kept me going full steam ahead. Thank you to my blood brother, Ramesh Ganeshram, and soul brother, Darrel Sukhdeo, for being careful readers and energetic cheerleaders. My gratitude is endless for my tireless agent, Michael Psaltis, who often sees the path clearer than I do. Many thanks to Chef Rob Bleifer, the captain at the helm of Food Network's test kitchens, for giving me the tour and chat that enabled me to write the in-studio and contest scenes in the book. What can I say about my friend, and one of my own culinary heroes, Daisy Martinez, for agreeing to let me make her a character in this book? Thank you a million times, Daisy, for all you do and for being who you are.

Gratitude to my husband, Jean Paul Vellotti, for believing in my work. Speaking of champions, no one is a greater cheerleader than my dear friend Monica Bhide, from whom great things always come.

Most of all, an infinity of thank-yous to my sweet daughter, Sophia Parvin Vellotti, for being my reason and passion to write and live.

Property of:
Henry County Library System
1001 Florence McGarity Blvd.
McDonough, GA 30252

Assigned to:
☒ Cochran Public Library
☐ Fairview Public Library
☐ Fortson Public Library
☐ Locust Grove Public Library
☐ McDonough Public Library